MW01504599

The Elites:
The Perfect Arrangement

A novel by
Regine Coney

The Elites: The Perfect Arrangement
by Regine Coney

ISBN-13: 9781073766512

Published by:
Emperial Publishing
P.O. Box 21402
Detroit, MI 48221
(313) 449-8543

Email: regine.coney21@icloud.com
Website: www.EmperialPublishing.com
First Printing: May 2019

Acknowledgements

It's finally here—my book! It has been a long journey for me. I wasn't exactly sure what I wanted to do in life. I just know I love to read and write, and now my dreams are reality.

Thank you, Tonja Ayers, for helping publish my first book.

Thank you also to Mom, Dad, and my big brother Korey for believing in me and listening to me talk about writing a book for years.

I'm enjoying this moment in my life. Thank You, God, for everything.

Love, Regine.

The Elites:
The Perfect Arrangement

Chapter One
The Founders Ball

Every year, Detroit, Michigan's, most elite men and women get all dressed up and to be awarded and honored for their accomplishments but most importantly, the work they have done for the city at The Founders Ball. Some of these elite people have built new buildings and given back to the community; others have just simply become millionaires by creating amazing brands and businesses. It is the most extraordinary and extravagant affair to attend in Michigan, and anyone who is known around Michigan attends the event. I attended because my best friend/business partner Karrine and myself were always invited for our clothing store Tags and Bags, and every year we've won an award for our business.

This time around I was quite overwhelmed. I had just gone through a bad break-up with my long-time boyfriend Danny. He and I hadn't been getting along for the past few months, and for some reason, we ended our relationship on the night of the ball. I had cried my eyes out and just wanted to stay home and drown in my own sorrow, but Karrine needed me more than ever this year. So, unfortunately, I had to suck it up and go to the event.

I glanced through my closet trying to find the right formal dress to wear. I picked out a long, black mermaid dress with a split that stopped at my upper thigh. I curled my hair to perfection, added a few extensions to give it more volume, then put on a little makeup to finish the look. As I looked in the mirror, admiring my beauty, my small hips fit the dress well, my boobs set up just right without a bra, and my almond skin tone went great with the dress. But, inside, I felt a little uneasy and unhappy; a small part of me still missed Danny. I wanted to work out my relationship with him, but he and I needed space.

My cellphone buzzed on my bed. I shuffled through the unmade sheets and grabbed it.

"Hello."

"Come on, Lauren. I'm outside in a black Tahoe. Hurry; I don't want to be late," Karrine said.

I rolled my eyes, grabbed my black clutch purse, swiftly put on my black open-toe four-inch heels, and walked out the door. The driver opened the right rear door for me and waited for me to get safely into the truck. Karrine and I embraced one another with a hug and smooches on the cheek.

Karrine and I met at Fairlane Mall ten years ago when we both were teenagers. Karrine was two years older than I. It was after nine o' clock and the mall had closed. I was waiting for my mother outside the mall by the AMC movie theater sitting on a huge rock. I'd repeatedly tried calling her, but she hadn't picked up. That was very common with my mother. I assumed she probably was out, sleeping around with some man—or someone else's man.

Karrine walked out the mall with a handful of shopping bags in both hands, noticed me sitting on the rock, and walked over to me. She asked me if I needed a ride home, and I said no. I was too embarrassed and ashamed to admit that my mother had forgotten about me. Karrine nodded and walked away, but fifteen minutes later she came back.

"Listen, I don't mind giving you a ride. I've been waiting in my car, watching you for like fifteen minutes," she said.

Karrine has always been very stylish and she keeps up with the latest fashions. Karrine stood in front of me with her Prada purse, keys dangling from her fresh acrylic nails, blue jean shorts, white tank top, and nude wedges that made her outfit stand out. I looked down at my black flip flops, old jeans, and Tupac t-shirt I'd worn over a dozen times. I felt small standing next to Karrine, but she didn't make me feel small. Karrine was nice and helpful, and honestly, I was surprised she was even talking to me. Boys and older men walked out the mall, and each one of them stared at Karrine from head to toe. Karrine rolled her eyes and looked back at me.

I looked both ways, hoping my mother would bend the corner, but she didn't. She was nowhere to be found.

"Okay... Cool... I live on Marlowe Street, right off Joy Road. If it's too far, I can wait on my mom," I blurted out, still feeling embarrassed.

"Come on, girl," she said.

"What's your name?" I asked.

"Karrine. What's your name?"

"Lauren."

Karrine had a silver four-door Toyota Camry that still had the new-car smell. She turned on some music and blasted the air as we drove away from Fairlane Mall. We pulled into a nearby Coney Island on Chicago and Greenfield, and she bought food for me. I was shocked because she really didn't even know me like that. She didn't ask me for money or anything. She just asked me what I wanted and covered the cost for me. After eating at the Coney Island, we pulled in front of my house and my mother's car was still there. I rolled my eyes and exhaled, annoyed that she'd forgotten about me again.

"Thanks, Karrine."

"No problem."

I heard a loud noise from my house and could hear my mother screaming at the top of her lungs. Karrine still sat outside, making sure I got in my house safety. Suddenly, the police pulled into our driveway. My heart started to race and I began to cry. The police took my mother and the random man to jail that night. All my neighbors were outside, and Karrine hurried out her car and rushed to my side. My mother didn't look at me. All she kept doing was yelling at the random man for cheating on her. The nerve of my mother. I'm her child, her only child, and she didn't even look at me.

An officer who had been talking to one of my neighbors pulled out a notepad and a pen. He started writing some notes, walked over to me and Karrine, then pulled out his cellphone and called the Child and Family Services Department. My eyes welled with tears and I begged the officer not to take me, but he was stern.

"Sorry, young lady, but you're under eighteen years old, and we can't have you home alone in the city of Detroit by yourself. It's the law," he said.

"Wait; I'm her older cousin Karrine. We were just at the mall and I'm eighteen years old," she said and pulled out her ID.

"Is this your older cousin?" he asked, looking at me.

I nodded yes, wiping my tears.

"All right; you take good care of her until her mother gets out next week," he said.

"Next week?" I asked.

"Yes. It's a Thursday night, and my partner and I won't be doing our paperwork until Friday. Monday is a holiday so your mother won't be able to see a judge until Tuesday or Wednesday; that's the way the system works. But you'll be fine; you have your cousin here," he said, walking away.

The officer didn't care. He took my mother away without any remorse or guilt. I guess my situation was just another case to him. I felt horrible and alone, and I didn't know what to do.

"Pack all your stuff up. You can stay with me; I have my own place. I'll drive you to school and help you out," Karrine said.

We arrived at Karrine's house in Allen Park. Karrine explained when her grandmother passed some years back, she'd left her a house and a lot of money. Once Karrine turned eighteen, she inherited a fabric business in Southfield from her grandmother. She was a fucking business owner at eighteen years old. It was absolutely astonishing.

Karrine and I bonded over our love for fashion. She loved my style, the way I dressed, and the way I did my hair. Karrine became my big sister, best friend, and guardian until I turned eighteen. She made sure I didn't go without anything. At first, I didn't understand why she was so nice and caring to me, but later on, I just decided to go with the flow. Ever since that day, Karrine and I had been inseparable.

Karrine was tall and petite with a pixie haircut, and she had golden caramel skin. She was absolutely stunning and men ate out the palm of her hand. Karrine was known for being a bitch at times, but she never showed that side to me.

"How are you holding up?" Karrine asked, fixing her makeup.

"Ummm... I'm hanging in there. Can't believe after five years of being with him, he would just up and leave," I said, looking out the window.

"Yeah, well, that's men, but you will find someone better than him."

I shrugged my shoulders, my eyes still glued to the traffic. Downtown Detroit was lit up. People were out walking the streets in their summer clothes, laughing, smiling, and enjoying the evening breeze as I sadly watched them in my ballgown on my way to one of the hottest events in Detroit.

"Lauren, I have some juicy shit to tell you."

I turned my head around and looked at her.

"Well, do you remember Queen? You know Queen; she's one of our clients who comes into Tags and Bags. She comes in almost every week and spends about a thousand on merchandise."

I tilted my head trying to remember the woman she was speaking about, but it was hard for me to recall her face. Plenty of women came in and out of the store. I could never remember them by name, only by their faces. I was always really good with faces, but not names.

"I don't remember her."

"Ugh, oh my goodness, Lauren, you need to remember her face. That's what makes the story better."

"Well, do you have a picture of her on social media or something?"

Karrine smirked and swiftly pulled out her cellphone. Once she showed me a picture of the woman, I finally remembered her. Queen was one of our regulars, and just like Karrine had said, she spent a lot of money at the store. Queen was a voluptuous and beautiful woman with freckles all over her face, and she had thick, black naturally curly hair that went to the middle of her back. Queen was married to a man named Jacob who was a business tycoon and was about ten years older than she. Rumor had it that Queen was a hoe who slept around with other businessmen and her husband had no clue about her affairs. That was the rumor I'd heard and that rumor had come from Karrine.

"Okay, yeah, I remember her. So, what's so juicy?"

Karrine smirked. "I'm having a little threesome with Queen and Jacob."

My mouth flew open, and I grabbed Karrine's cellphone out her hand and looked at the picture closely.

"These two? Get the hell outta here! Really?!" I asked in awe.

Karrine nodded her head.

"When did you find the time to have this little affair with them? And, why am I now, finding out about it?"

Karrine started to laugh. "I mean, I just didn't want you to judge me, so I lied. I have the perfect arrangement with those two."

I started to smile in disbelief. "So... you're actually sleeping with both of them... like, for real?"

"Yes, whenever they're in the mood for my company, Queen calls me. Sometimes, it's here in Michigan; other times, Jacob flies me and Queen out. We've been to Las Vegas, the Bahamas, Miami, Los Angles, Texas, Atlanta, and Arizona," she explained with excitement.

"K, we've been to all those places before, and it's been on our dime. Why are you acting like you've never been?" I asked, confused.

Karrine rolled her eyes. "I mean, yeah, but those were all business trips to expand our store or to meet up with business partners about stock. But, when I'm with them, it's all fun and games."

I chuckled. "Okay, K."

"I mean, Lauren, what's so wrong with having sex with two married adults? They are rich and powerful, and they're on my level, reputation wise. I mean, really, Lauren, what could possibly go wrong?"

"You're right; I'm sorry. Tell me more."

Karrine continued with her sex-crazed and exciting stories about her affair with Queen and Jacob. Finally, we arrived at The Founders Ball at The Magnificent Hotel on Cass Avenue. There were reporters and journalists outside, people taking plenty of pictures, and as we stepped out on the red carpet, all eyes were on us.

Karrine and I walked the carpet together, and she and I took plenty of pictures and spoke to a lot of the other entrepreneurs and other elite people of our social standard. Including, the mayor of Detroit, who Karrine and I had a great business relationship with. Once we were in the hotel, Karrine and I went our separate ways. She walked through the ball, while I sat at the bar. I took two shots of tequila and one shot of Hennessy. Surprisingly, I felt good; I didn't feel drunk or tipsy. I pulled out my cellphone and looked at Danny's number for about fifteen minutes. I contemplated whether I should or shouldn't text him.

I wanted more than anything to speak to him. I wondered if he was thinking about me the way I was thinking about him, but my pride got the best of me. I put my cellphone back into my purse and walked around the venue. After speaking to a few people, I got bored and walked out the ball into the lobby. I sat on the sofa and watched the guests roam around the expensive and extravagant hotel.

Chapter Two
A Night to Remember

"Now, don't you look bored?"

I looked over and there was a handsome man standing across from me. He wore a navy-blue three-piece suit and was tall, with broad shoulders, light brown eyes, and an amazing caramel skin tone.

"I'm Drew, and you're...?" he asked.

"Lauren," I replied, in a nonchalant tone.

I knew exactly who Drew was. He had done a lot for Detroit. He had been in the news for giving back to schools and to neighborhoods as well. Drew was one of Michigan's top business tycoons—well-dressed, well-liked, and very powerful. Drew was much older than I; he had to be in his late thirties, but he didn't look like it at all.

"Well, Lauren, why are you sitting out here?"

I squinted my eyes and smirked. "Not really in the mood for fake laughs tonight."

I rose to my feet. "Excuse me, I have to go to the ladies' room," I said, walking away from Drew.

Although Drew was handsome and charming, I wasn't interested in him or anyone. I walked in the ladies' room and walked right back out; surprisingly, when I bent the corner, Drew was standing outside waiting for me. I walked past him as if I didn't see him. He started to follow me and called out my name.

"Lauren... Lauren..."

I stopped in my tracks and turned around to him. "What?!"

"Damn! Why are you so evil?"

I smirked.

"Oh, there we go. We have a winner, ladies and gentlemen. She smiled," he said, teasing me.

"Look, you seem very sweet and endearing, but I just got out of a relationship and I'm in no mood to chitchat," I said, blowing him off.

Drew smirked and nodded his head, put both hands in his pockets, and shook his head. A woman walked up to Drew; she was drop-dead gorgeous. She resembled an Instagram model, and she appeared to have had plastic surgery. Her boobs were popping out of her dress which stopped at her upper thigh. She wearing very high heels and a long black weave that stopped at her butt. The woman whispered in Drew's ear, and as she whispered, she touched his chest. Drew seemed embarrassed by the woman. He cleared his throat and gently removed her hand from his chest.

I shook my head and snickered at Drew; then I simply walked away from him. Drew walked behind me, leaving the woman.

"Sorry, Lauren. She and I met a few nights back," he tried explaining.

"You don't have to explain anything to me, Drew. It's okay. It was nice chatting with you, but I have to go. Enjoy your night."

This time he didn't follow me and I was so thankful he didn't. I thought it was bold of him to walk up to me, but I wasn't interested at all. I walked back into the event and scanned the room looking for Karrine; she was talking to Queen. Unlike Karrine, I wasn't intrigued by Queen's social stand in Detroit. Most men and women were, but to me, she was a just another regular chick, who married a man with money. Typical.

"Okay, so this is going to be a long night," I mumbled to myself.

Karrine walked over to me, then she and I went over to our assigned table near the front of the stage where the mayor would give out the awards. I sipped champagne as I scoped out the room. Karrine went on about Queen and Jacob and how they had plans to meet up after the event. I listened as she went on and on. Drew walked over to our table. I cleared my throat and sat up straight in my seat, feeling a little annoyed. He was so aggravating. Did he not get the picture? I didn't want to be bothered, yet he wouldn't just leave me the hell alone. My eyes darted to him as he fixed his suit and sat down.

"Are you really going to keep following me like this?" I asked.

Drew smirked and lifted the place card that had been put on the table by the hotel associates. Drew had ironically been assigned to the same table as I had, as had Queen and Jacob.

As Jacob pulled out Queen's seat, the woman who had walked up to Drew in the lobby sat directly next to him. I felt so stupid.

"Oh, sorry... I didn't know," I said, feeling embarrassed.

He nodded and started talking to Jacob.

"Why are you being a bitch toward him?" Karrine whispered.

"The son-of-a-bitch kept following me out in the lobby. I thought he was following me around again. Sorry," I whispered back.

"Well, relax. He's Jacob's business partner, so don't piss him off."

"No; tell him not to piss *me* off."

Karrine and I chuckled.

The mayor walked up to the podium and the room became quiet. The mayor started to talk about the city of Detroit and how much it had grown. I tuned the mayor out and looked around the table. As the woman whispered in Drew's ear, his eyes were glued on me. For a moment, he and I stared at one another; our attention was interrupted when the mayor called him on the stage for his award.

The room cheered and clapped for Drew as he walked up to the stage and to the podium. Drew gave an astounding speech and thanked his business partner Jacob for believing in him and helping him with his business. The night went on and Karrine and I were honored as well, and we received money for our charity as well. After an hour of speakers, awards, and champagne toasts, The Founders Ball was over. I was so tired. I walked out the ball and waited for Karrine. She walked up to me with a smile on her face.

"Oh no! You've got something up your sleeve," I said.

"Jacob and Drew rented out all three penthouse suites for us on the top floor. Jacob and Queen have one, Drew has one, and you and I will have one to ourselves."

"Oh no, I'm just going to go home. I'm tired and I've embarrassed myself enough," I said, walking away.

Karrine grabbed my arm and gave me puppy dog eyes.

"No, K; I already embarrassed myself in front of the entire table, and I know that guy Drew must think I'm a bitch. I literally made him look like a stalker. There's no way I'm staying in the suite he paid for. Absolutely not!"

"Come on, Lauren. For me... please? I want to share this moment with you. We won and we have a chance to stay at this five-star hotel for free. After my nightcap with Jacob and Queen, I'll come back to our suite and explain the whole night. It will be fun. We can order room service and talk about Danny, and I can tell you all about my sex-crazed night."

I exhaled. "Okay, but make sure you come back."

Karrine and I stepped off the elevator on the sixtieth floor. The floor was huge and there were only three doors on the floor. Karrine and I shared suite 608. Our suite had four rooms; it was really nice and lavish. Karrine jumped in the shower then rushed over to Jacob and Queen's suite, 607.

I roamed around the suite, starting to get bored. I walked out on the balcony and watched as cars drove past the hotel. I glanced at the clock. It was only midnight on a Saturday night, so a lot of people were walking the streets of downtown Detroit. Those driving were blasting their music, and some of the people walking around were completely drunk.

My stomach growled, so I decided to change into one of the white, fluffy comfortable robes and order room service. I grabbed the ice bucket, and when I opened my suite door, I saw Drew kissing the woman from the ball. The woman stared at me in confusion; she seemed slightly jealous that I was in a comfortable robe while she was being sent off into the night. I walked past both of them with the ice bucket close to my chest and my head down. I'd already embarrassed myself enough; I couldn't even look Drew in the eye.

"Are you sure you don't want me to stay?" the insecure woman asked.

"No, love; I have a lot of work to catch up on," he replied.

I heard the elevator doors close as I bent the corner. I got my ice and was planning to wait at least five minutes before walking back to my suite. I couldn't risk bumping into Drew again; I couldn't face him yet. As I waited quietly like a dog with its tail tucked, Drew bent the corner, crossed his arms, and chuckled at me.

"I'm not mad at you, Lauren."

I exhaled with relief. It was a good thing he didn't take my attitude toward him earlier personal. I mean, it seemed that

Drew was a good guy. I was feeling a little guilty and decided to give him the benefit of doubt.

"I'm sorry. I shouldn't have gone off on you like that. I was being a brat earlier," I explained.

"You're fine."

Drew looked me up and down. His eyes were soft and he had lust in his eyes. I didn't understand what he was lusting after. I had on a huge white robe and white slippers. There was nothing sexy or appealing about me at that moment.

"Well, I just ordered room service. It should be here soon. I'm going to go back to my room now."

"Can I eat with you?" he asked.

I squinted my eyes and crossed my arms. "Here you go, back on your bullshit."

We both burst out laughing.

"I just want to get to know you," he replied.

His response seemed sincere, and we went back to his suite where he ordered room service for himself. After another thirty minutes, when our food arrived, we were laughing and talking. The more I talked to Drew, I realized how endearing and genuine he truly was. I'd thought I had him figured out. I'd thought he was brash and arrogant, but he wasn't at all; he had a humble soul. He talked about how he'd grown up in a rough neighborhood and how he was only thirteen years old when he saw his older brother get shot in front of him on the east side of Detroit.

I leaned into Drew and kissed him on his lips. When I pulled back, he leaned in and kissed me. This time our tongues met and intertwined with one another. Drew started to untie the belt on my robe and to unzip his pants. My mind was telling me to stop, but my body had complete control. Without any hesitation, Drew pulled down my panties and started to lick and touch my clit. My eyes rolled to the back of my head. I pushed Drew's head deeper and deeper, and after a few more minutes, I came. Drew removed his pants then pulled out a condom. We stared each other in the eyes for a moment. When Drew slid his dick into me, I moaned. Drew thrusted in and out of me, leaving me wanting and craving more. Drew and I came at the same time, and once we'd released all the tension and lust from our systems, we lay on the sofa holding each other. I fell asleep on his chest.

I awakened the next morning in Drew's bed, the sheets undone, and I was completely naked. I leaned up and scanned the room. I heard the shower running in the bathroom and assumed Drew was in there. I hurried and seized my white robe from the sofa and swiftly left Drew's room without saying goodbye. I rushed over to the room Karrine and I were staying in and hurried and closed the door behind me. When I turned around, I saw two women cleaning our room.

"The room is being cleaned, ma'am," one of them said.

"Huh? This is my room; my friend and I are staying here," I replied.

"Yes, ma'am; however, checkout for room 608 was at eleven o' clock this morning and it's twelve-thirty now."

I bit my bottom lip, feeling embarrassed.

"I'm guessing that dress over there is yours," she said, pointing to the dress in the trash bin.

The other woman snickered and shook her head. "Somebody had too much to drink, I see," she mumbled.

I rolled my eyes, grabbed my dress and purse from the trash bin and went into the bathroom to put back on my gown. I swiftly pulled out my cellphone and called Karrine.

"Where-the-hell are you?" I asked.

"I've been looking for you. I'm downstairs in the lobby. Hurry!" she replied.

I walked out the hotel suite feeling ashamed; it was quite embarrassing for those women to see me like that. I felt like I was doing the ultimate walk of shame. My hair was a complete disaster and I was wearing the same gown I'd had on yesterday. I'd gone from class to trash in less than twenty-four hours. I approached Karrine, who had on a summer dress, her hair freshly curled, and her makeup freshly beat.

"Wow! Look at you. You look great, while I look like trash," I said.

"Jacob took us shopping," she replied with a smile.

"Please, get me the hell out of here."

"Okay; go freshen up. I ordered another room and grabbed you something new; Jacob purchased it for you. While you go do that, let me check us out of 608," she said, handing me the key and a shopping bag.

I hurried and showered, got dressed, and came back; Karrine was still checking us out.

"This bitch must be new," Karrine whispered to me.

I chuckled. "Be nice, K."

I gave Karrine my key to the room, and she approached the desk. As I glanced around the beautiful hotel, I saw Drew getting off the elevator. I felt my heart drop to my stomach, and for a moment, I couldn't breathe. I rushed over to Karrine and told her we had to go immediately. Karrine and I were seconds from walking out the door—when Karrine and I bumped into a woman.

"Hey, Danielle," Karrine said, speaking to the woman.

"Hey, Karrine. How are you?" she asked.

"Good. What about you?" Karrine asked.

"Oh, just here stopping by to see my husband, Drew," she said.

My eyes widened and I felt my heart thumping uncontrollably. That was when my worst fear happened. Drew walked up to Danielle and embraced her with a hug and a kiss on her lips. Danielle had a heart-shaped face, black hair that stopped at her shoulders, curvy hips, and brown skin that glowed in the sunlight.

"Hey, babe," he said.

Drew looked at me with no emotion. He took Danielle's hand and smiled at me as if it was his first time meeting me. I simply nodded; this was so damn embarrassing. Karrine and I walked over to the Tahoe and the driver opened the door for us.

Once I was home, I took a hot bath and decided not to go into Tags and Bags. I wanted to relax and reflect on my actions. I felt so stupid and embarrassed that I actually had sympathy for Drew. And I felt even worse that I'd had sex with him. I knew better, but dammit, his dick was well needed last night.

"What a fucking night to remember," I mumbled to myself.

Chapter Three
Wife or Not

Finally, things were back to normal. I was back at the store working and styling my clients for dates, weddings, out-of-town vacations, and just normal everyday wear. Karrine hadn't been in the store the whole week. She would call me and text me to let me know she was either with Queen and Jacob, or just Queen. After a while, I started not to care. Karrine was a grown-ass woman, and she was capable of doing whatever she wanted, whenever and with whomever she desired.

As I roamed around the store cleaning and organizing, I saw a familiar face walk into the store. It was Danielle. I tried my best not to stare and I tried my best to keep my distance, but she approached me.

"Are you Lauren?" she asked.

"Yes," I said nonchalantly.

"I'm Drew's wife."

"Okay. Is that supposed to faze me or excite me?"

She smirked. "It should. I mean, you're the hoe who slept with him; am I correct?"

"What the hell are you talking about?"

"Oh, you know what I'm talking about. The Founders Ball, Lauren, when he and Jacob rented out one of the suites for you, and you and him fucked that night. Ring a bell yet?"

"Be very careful with your words. I don't want to make a mistake and knock your ass out."

Danielle folded her arms and leaned against the wall. The sale associates and clients in the store all stared at us as Danielle and I stared each other down.

"Can we talk in private?" she asked.

I nodded and led her to the back to the office Karrine and I shared together. Danielle sat down in one of the chairs and I sat behind the desk. We stared at each other for a few minutes.

"Okay... So, are you gone to talk because I have a store to run?" I said.

"Listen, I don't know you and you sure as fuck don't know me. I have eyes and ears everywhere around this city, and anything that involves Drew I know about it. I don't care if you're fucking my husband because I'm reaping the financial benefits of my marriage. Just make sure you keep your mouth shut. Drew is a very rich and powerful man, and he has a reputation to maintain."

"Bitch, I don't want your husband. I didn't know he was married because, if I had, I wouldn't have even looked in his direction."

Danielle chuckled. "Please, save that shit for one of these other housewives. Like I said before, you can have your fun with my husband, but just know your place. Keep his name out of the media, don't tell any of your friends, and most importantly, don't tell him I know about your little affair!" she demanded.

"Girl, please," I said as I rose to my feet.

"Look I'm doing you a favor. At least I'm letting you get a taste of him, but remember, I'm one of the elites now, and what I say goes. So, listen, and there will be no consequences."

"Bitch, please don't act like you're sparing my life because you aren't! Get the hell out of my store."

"You know how many women I've come across who fed me the same lies you are now? Plenty! So, forgive me for not having sympathy for you. Just do us all a favor and make sure you keep your affair with Drew under wraps because, frankly, if it leaks out, I don't have time to clean up the mess." She said, sternly.

Danielle grabbed her purse and walked out the store. I was pissed with Drew for not telling me he was married! I was confused about how Danielle knew Drew and I had been together that night. I hadn't even told Karrine I'd slept with Drew, so how in the hell had it gotten out? I looked out the window, brushing off the thought of Drew and Danielle. I wasn't going to see Drew ever again, so there was no reason to even investigate who'd ran their mouth.

Karrine came walking through the door with a hangover, wearing huge black sunglasses. She threw her purse down on the desk and sat on the black sofa in the office. I shook my head and chuckled, and Karrine looked over at me and smiled.

"Shut those blinds, all that damn sun coming through," she said.

"I thought you weren't coming in today."

"I wasn't, but I haven't been in all week. I felt like I was neglecting the business. Take the rest of the day off; I've got everything under control."

I crossed my arms. "Karrine, go home. You have a hangover."

"No, I'm fine, but I have some great news. Queen is having a dinner party tonight, so we have to find some really cute dresses."

"Oh, hell no, not again! Especially if that loser Drew is going to be there."

Karrine looked at me confused. She still didn't know about me sleeping with Drew, so she didn't understand my frustration toward him. She took off her huge sunglasses and stared at me.

"What's so wrong with Drew? He's a good guy and he's very nice by the way too."

"Nothing, nothing at all. I'm just saying, he was following me all around The Founders Ball last week, and he has a wife. Ugh, girl, I'm just not feeling his thirsty ass."

Karrine burst out laughing.

"I know you aren't talking about that lunatic Danielle! They aren't legally married, Lauren. Drew just gave her a ring to shut her up. The woman is delusional. She walks around and calls herself his wife, but Drew doesn't claim her as his wife."

"What?! Then why her crazy ass claiming she's married?"

"Yes, she is nuts! Don't get me wrong, Drew may really like her and maybe he might care, but he is definitely not wifing her."

"And how do you know all of this?"

"Queen."

"Of course, Queen. Keep your eye on her; she seems a little cunning to me. Isn't Danielle supposed to be her girl? I see them together in pictures on social media all the time, and now she's just spilling that girl's tea. Aren't they supposed to be Michigan's finest? Only hanging out with women with rings and husbands, blah, blah, blah?" I said, teasing.

Karrine shook her head. "Be nice, Queen is my friend... She's our friend."

"That bitch is not my friend, and don't be surprised if she does something deceitful."

Karrine walked out the office and I followed behind her to finish cleaning the store. Karrine stopped in her tracks and turned her body completely around to look at me.

"What?" I asked, confused.

"Take the rest of the day off. I'll be at your place at eight to pick you up."

"I'm not going. Did you not hear me back there?"

Karrine brushed past me, grabbed my keys and purse, and held my hand all the way out the door to my BMW. She opened the door, gently pushed me in the car, and gave me a kiss on the cheek.

"Go home. You've worked hard enough this week. Oh, and make sure your outfit is cute. We have to turn heads tonight."

I drove straight home, and when I arrived, I saw flowers on my porch. I walked onto the porch, picked up the beautiful red roses, and opened my front door. I opened the white envelope, pulled out the bright red card, and saw written in black ink at the bottom:

Sorry, I still love you and I will always love you.
Love
Danny

I put the red roses in a vase and sat them near the window in the kitchen so they could have sunlight. I thought about how alluring and thoughtful the roses were. I'd thought I would never hear from Danny again, let alone receive roses from him. He and I had ended very badly. Our relationship had started to get so toxic toward the end that I knew there was no possible way to rekindle our love.

I took a nice long bath and roamed around the house afterward, cleaning and talking on the phone with a friend. That's when I heard a knock at my door. I swiftly ran toward the door, peeked out the window, and saw Danny's black-on-black F150 in front of my house. I tapped my freshly manicured nails against my waist and shook my head in disbelief.

"I can't catch a fucking break," I mumbled.

I hung up the phone with my friend and heard another knock at my door; this time it was much more aggressive.

"WHO IS IT?" I yelled out, being silly.

"Lauren, now you know it's me out here," he said in his deep voice.

"Sorry, I don't know someone named *me*," I said, being a tease.

"Come on, Lauren, please; just let me talk really quick."

I shrugged my shoulders and swung the door open. The nice summer breeze hit my face. Danny stood in my doorway with another bouquet of red roses in his hand. He hadn't missed a beat; he still looked and smelled amazing. He had on grey sweatpants, a white fitted tee, and black sneakers. His beard and hair were freshly groomed, his smile still bright, his eyes honey brown, and his brown skin glowed in the sunlight. I could smell his cologne as the breeze blew, and at that moment, I wanted to take him in my bedroom and have sex with him.

"What do you want?" I asked.

"I've missed you. I just got finished closing a deal on one of the houses in Detroit, and I wanted to stop by and check on you."

I looked Danny up and down, and knew he was being dishonest. Danny never wore chill clothes to close a business deal; he would normally be dressed appropriately, sometimes in a suit and other times in black slacks and a button-up.

"You're lying to me. You closed a deal with that on?" I said, pointing at his clothes.

"All right, so I didn't close a deal; maybe I just wanted to come see you."

I tilted my head to the right and smiled. Danny seemed very profound and he was the only man I'd ever loved. Breaking up and making up had been the pattern for our relationship. He and I were toxic when we were around one another, and although I'd made a huge mistake by sleeping with Drew, I thought it would be doltish of me to take Danny back. Danny and I were always on a rollercoaster; he and I didn't have any balance. Since he'd been gone, I'd found balance in myself. I'd realized I didn't need Danny in my life. I was perfectly fine without him.

"Let's give it one more shot," he said.

Typical Danny, always wanting to give it another shot, but I was done giving shots. I needed foundation and stability in a man. I didn't want to be in a toxic relationship nor did I want to be in a relationship that was always up and down. I wanted some kind of balance, and Danny had shown me more than once that he wasn't capable of doing the job.

"Maybe not this time," I replied.

"What? What do you mean, Lauren? Are you really giving up on us?"

I bit my bottom lip and my eyes welled with tears. I guess so."

Danny's honey brown eyes widened, and as I looked into his eyes, I could see the hurt I'd caused. Then his eyes welled with tears, and he nodded, placed the bouquet of roses on my porch, and walked away. I shut the door. I couldn't watch him leave in his truck; it was too painful.

Later, that night, I got dressed for the dinner party for Queen, and as I got dressed, I only thought of Danny. I thought I'd made a huge mistake by not taking him back. It was exactly six-thirty and Karrine was outside. This time she didn't have a driver; she was driving her black Bentley. As Karrine and I rode to Queen's dinner, Karrine talked about Queen and Jacob. I tuned her out. I was so tired of hearing about Queen and Jacob. It seemed like lately all she talked about was those two.

"When do you think this little affair will end?" I asked.

"Ummm... You know, I never thought about it."

"Don't you want your own man? Like a real relationship, not sleeping with a couple all the time?"

"I mean, I've had my share of bad relationships, and this is all fun and games right now. You're in no position to judge me, Lauren."

"I'm not judging."

"Please; you are judging me right now. And to add salt to the wound, you didn't even tell me about you and Drew on the night of The Founders Ball."

I turned my head to Karrine and she smirked.

"Oh, you thought I wasn't gone to notice you were gone?" she said, then burst out laughing.

"How do you know about that?"

Karrine pulled into the parking lot and parked her car; we were at the restaurant for Queen's dinner. I turned my head and saw Queen arrive in a black Tahoe then walk inside with Danielle next to her.

"You have got to be fucking kidding me!"

Karrine grinned and nodded her head.

"Let me guess, Queen opened her big mouth?" I said.

"Bingo! Queen told me she saw you and Drew talking in the lobby, and later on that night, she saw you go into his hotel room. Then she said the following morning she went over to talk to him and saw you in the bed naked."

My mouth flew open as Karrine gave me the run down. "Sneaky, bitch." I said.

"Sneaky? You're the sneaky bitch. Why didn't you tell me?"

"Because it was just a one-night thing. It wasn't going to turn into anything other than that. I promise you; Queen is always running her mouth."

"Come on, Lauren, let's make the best out of this night."

"Fine, but if that bitch Danielle says anything disrespectful, I will slap the shit out of her."

Karrine burst out laughing.

"Relax." she said.

Chapter Four
Liar, Liar, Part One

The host greeted us then told us to follow her to Queen's dinner party that was upstairs, all the way in the back, looking over the Detroit Riverwalk. Queen embraced Karrine with a hug then turned to me and gave me a hug. When I hugged Queen, something was off. It didn't seem sincere, it seemed fake and forced, but I played along with her. I didn't want to make a scene or seem like a bitch at her party. I couldn't understand why Karrine trusted and liked Queen so much; she was so fraudulent and conniving. Karrine was giving Queen a fair chance, but I wasn't; I was keeping a close eye on her. Nothing about her was sweet or beguile. She walked around like she was on some kind of high horse simply because she was one of the elites.

The round table where we all sat held about twenty people and all of them were elites except for Karrine and me. I knew Karrine was going to make sure she and I were next on the list, but I didn't care about being an elite. They were all stuck up, snotty, and impertinent. As the three waiters who were assisting our table brought the food and poured drinks, every last one of the elites at the table treated the waiters like servants—very rude, demanding, haughty, and impatient. They were all like Queen, and as I watched all of it play out, I couldn't help but wonder why Karrine wanted to be part of the elite clique so bad. We had decent lives, lived well, and had money sitting in our bank accounts. What was so special about being an elite?

When Karrine and I sat down, I didn't glance around the room; I kept my eyes locked on the menu. I didn't want to see Drew or his insane *wannabe*-wife, but the waiter approached me and I had no choice but to look up. When I did, Drew was gazing at me. I glared at him then turned to my waiter. As I glanced around the table, I saw Danielle sitting next to Karrine instead of Drew. I was a little confused by it, but I didn't pay it any mind.

An hour passed and I had to go to the ladies' room. I walked out the back of the restaurant, down the corridor to the ladies' room. After flushing the toilet, I washed my hands, and when I looked up, Danielle was standing behind me.

"Oh, it's the crazy wannabe-wife," I said.

"So funny; just know your place," she replied.

I rolled my eyes and turned around to Danielle. It was so pathetic of her to keep following me around, pressing me about a man I didn't want. Danielle was very jealous of me and she was insecure.

"You're so pathetic," I said.

"Excuse me?"

"You're pathetic. You're following me around like a lost puppy over a man I have no intentions of pursuing. Plus, bitch, you aren't even his wife. I know he only gave you that ring to shut you the fuck up, and yet, your ass is steady barking. Why won't you just shut the fuck up?"

"Kiss my ass."

I started to chuckle because it was actually comical how hard this woman was trying to belong. She craved the lifestyle Queen lived and she wanted to be so much like her. I could see it was eating her alive; she was losing her grip. She was afraid I would take her spot and she was worried that Drew possibly wanted me. And he did. But what she failed to realize was Drew and I had shared one night together and that was it.

"You don't know shit about me or Drew," she said.

"You want to be like Queen so bad; you want that life. You're a grown ass woman crying out in desperation for a man who doesn't want you. What, you want to be Detroit's royal couple? You want to be at the meet and greets, the mayor's home, shaking hands and kissing babies like Queen? News flash, sweetie, he doesn't want you. So it doesn't matter how many times you suck his dick or fuck him, he still doesn't want you. Let that sink in."

I grabbed my clutch and walked out the ladies' room, pulled out my cellphone, and texted Karrine to let her know I was going to the bar. I ordered a shot of tequila to loosen up a little. I was starting to get annoyed with the group of people Karrine kept bringing me around. While at the bar, I was approached by a bartender who was absolutely breathtaking—almond skin, brown natural curls that stopped at her shoulders, very tall, and slim. Although she looked amazingly beautiful, the woman looks like she was in her early thirties.

"I see you got tired of the bougie squad too," she said, taking a shot of tequila with me.

I nodded my head and she poured me another shot of tequila.

"I'm guessing they come here a lot and annoy the shit out all you guys working here," I said.

"Actually, no, they don't come here a lot. It's very rare when they come here."

"So, how do you know they're the bougie people? I mean, I can point out a select few," I said, chuckling.

"Queen and her little follower Danielle?"

"Spot on. Cheers to that," I said, and we both cheered with our shot glasses. "What's your name?"

"Keithly. What about you?"

"I'm Lauren. So, how do you know those bitches?"

"Well, that, my dear, is a long story, but we have time. I met Queen here some time back. She was very sweet and humble back then. Queen use to work here as a bartender about five years ago; she and I were like sisters. Same birthday and age; we're both thirty-nine."

"Shut up. You don't look that age and neither does she."

"I know. We used to get that a lot—good genes—but back to the story. She met Jacob here, and he wined and dined her with gifts, trips, money, and jewelry, but once he put a ring on her finger, she changed. She became very bougie and high maintenance and cut me off because I wasn't one of the elites like her. She stopped coming here, and that's why it is quite odd that she's here now."

"Well, happy birthday, since you guys share the same birthday."

Keithly smiled and poured me another shot of tequila. "This one's on the house."

"Cheers."

I found it quite compelling that Keithly felt comfortable enough to tell me about her past with Queen, but the story didn't surprise me. Queen was fake and I could tell that right off the bat. She wanted everything to be about her, and Karrine was falling for her little sham.

"Well, I'd better get back upstairs," I said, getting off the barstool.

Keithly looked at me. "Before you go, I have to make you aware of something. Don't underestimate Queen's actions. I know it may seem like she has it all together, but she doesn't. Queen plays the sweet and nice role, but don't be mistaken, she'll stab you right in the back with no remorse or regret. She is a sneaky and conniving bitch, and she'll do anything to get what she wants, trust me." She said, sternly.

Keithly eyes were wide and she seemed very serious. I didn't know why, but I knew Queen was sly and I knew she tried to play the innocent role. But the way Keithly spoke about her made it seem like Queen was a menacing woman.

"What did she do to you?"

Keithly glanced around the room then looked back at me.

"Jacob and Queen met here when she used to bartend. Jacob liked Queen a lot, and they started messing around. But before Jacob and Queen got married, there was another woman in Jacob's life, her name was Porsha. I don't know how or when Jacob met Porsha, but he really liked her. Porsha was his main squeeze, and during that time, Queen was his side piece. Of course, Queen didn't like that; she was so envious of Porsha. Whenever Jacob was upset with Queen, he would bring Porsha here to make her jealous. Queen's blood would boil every time she saw Porsha here. Then Queen befriended Porsha and they actually became really cool, but after a few months of Queen, Porsha, and Jacob's little merry-go-round, Porsha came up missing. Her body was found in the Detroit River."

My eyes widened and I sat back down on the stool. "You think Queen killed her?"

"No, but I do think Queen hired someone to kill Porsha; she wanted her life so badly. She wanted to be on Jacob's arm and at press conferences and dining at the most lavish and expensive places. She wanted that life and now she has it."

"What about Porsha? Did the cops know Porsha and Jacob were messing around? I mean, you did say she was at all these A-list functions. No one questioned Jacob about it?"

Keithly took another shot and offered me more, but I was pretty shook. I wanted to have a clear head when getting some juicy and mouthwatering tea like this.

"Jacob is a tycoon. He was born with a silver spoon in his mouth. His parents owned many businesses in Michigan. So, with his parents' money, plus his own combined, Jacob was able to pay a lot of shit off. He was able to keep the press and the police quiet because he's cool with a lot of them. So, again, be careful."

"What do you know about Drew?"

She smiled and crossed her arms. "Ahh, so Drew has charmed you away," she said, teasing me.

"Hell no; it's just he's always around. What's his story?"

"Well, I don't know much about Drew. The only thing I know is Jacob helped him with his businesses and now they're partners. He looked out for him and believed in his business-driven skills. Now he's one of the elites in Detroit. I do know Danielle has her claws in him; she wants him so badly. I see you might want him too."

Keithly leaned in closer and smirked at me. "Don't get caught up. You seem like a really sweet girl. All those elite Detroit people are crooked and twisted, willing to throw anybody under the bus. Mark my words, sweetie, get out while you can."

Drew walked up to the bar and looked at me. Keithly smirked and gave Drew a dab on his right-hand fist.

"Long time, no see, Keithly. How have you been, love?" he asked.

"Just fine. Just talking to my friend here. Sorry, sweetie, I didn't get your name."

"Lauren," I replied.

"Lauren? Right; I'm Keithly."

I caught what Keithly was doing. She was trying to throw Drew off by introducing herself to me again.

"I was talking to Lauren about Los Angeles and how I would love to go some day."

"Oh, I bet you were," he replied.

Keithly poured Drew a shot of tequila and placed it next to him.

"Now, you know I don't drink that weak shit," he said.

"My apology. Hennessy would do you well, right?"

When Keithly placed the shot of Hennessy next to Drew, the tension was so thick I could cut it with a knife. It made me uneasy and uncomfortable the way Keithly was acting. She seemed timorous and she was trying to hide her fear with humor and awkward jesters to make Drew feel more comfortable, but the look in Drew's eyes made me feel he wasn't taking her weird kindness well. It seemed he saw right through her, as if he knew she'd been talking shit about the elite people and spreading their business.

A mysterious man walked up to Drew and tapped him on the shoulder. Drew turned around and embraced the man with a hug. The man was handsome, tall and slim but with muscles, hair slicked back, and he wore a black suit. He resembled someone who was possibly in the mafia, and he had an accent like he was from New York or New Jersey.

"Let's talk business," Drew insisted.

But before this man could turn around, he and I locked eyes.

"Who is this beautiful woman?" he asked Drew.

Drew looked back and smiled.

The man approached me. "What's your name?" he asked with his accent.

"Lauren," I replied.

"Very beautiful name for a very gorgeous woman. I'm Ronnie; nice to meet you."

"Likewise," I replied.

Drew gently pulled Ronnie away from me.

"She's a good girl; let her enjoy her night," Drew said, walking away with Ronnie.

Keithly placed her hands on the bar. Her hands were shaking and her eyes were full of fear and regret. Keithly took another shot, but this time it was a shot of Hennessy. Keithly wiped her face then walked off, headed straight to the ladies' room on the first floor. I trailed behind her to make sure she was okay. I opened the ladies' room door then locked it behind Keithly and me. Keithly was in one of the stalls throwing up. I could hear her gagging and choking, then she started to cry. I knocked on the door to let her know I was there to help.

"Go away," she insisted.

"Keithly, come out here now and talk to me."

"No, I can't. I already fucked up. I should have just kept my mouth closed. He saw right through me."

"Who?"

"Drew," she said, pushing the door open. She walked over to the sink to rinse off her hands and wipe her mouth.

"You need to relax." I grabbed Keithly and walked her over to one of the comfy sofas in the ladies' room. "Relax."

Keithly was crying, but at that point, I didn't know if it was just the shots of tequila sneaking up on her.

"You don't understand. I know these people; they're dangerous. Drew must have been watching me speak to you; he is no fool."

"No, he didn't; relax. Drew was minding his own business and walked up to us, trying to be nosy. That's all."

"Be careful around them, Lauren."

Keithly fixed her makeup in the mirror then walked out the ladies' room. I exhaled and shook my head in disbelief. I was weary, drained, and a little tipsy. I was ready to go home. I walked out the ladies' room and back upstairs to the dinner party. When I arrived, Karrine was drunk and slurring her words. I grabbed Karrine and told her we were leaving, but she wanted to stay. She wanted to go mess around with Jacob and Queen. As soon as she said that, my mind wandered back to what Keithly had told me about Porsha.

I couldn't risk something bad happening to Karrine; I would be devastated. Queen was up to something; I just couldn't put my finger on it. Something wasn't right, something was off. Queen walked over to Karrine and me and wrapped her arm around my neck.

"Let's go to the after party, ladies."

Queen wasn't as drunk as Karrine was; Karrine was completely wasted.

"No; we're going to call it a night. I'm tired and Karrine is drunk."

Queen removed her arm from around my neck and grimaced at me. I peered my eyes, and she fixed her face with a fake smile.

"Okay. See you both soon, I guess."

Karrine and I wobbled our way to her car. I put Karrine in the car and we drove off. I decided to just go to my house instead of dropping Karrine off at her house. I laid her down in my guest bedroom and put a bucket by the side of the bed, grabbed my laptop, and googled the girl Porsha. Nothing really came up about the woman; all the blogs and websites about her were very vague. I looked at her Facebook page and went through her pictures and her statuses. She was so pretty and young; she was a college graduate who'd majored in science.

I checked all her family's pages and close friends' pages; nothing seemed off about Porsha to me. From the pictures and posts on her Facebook page, she was very close to her parents. The deeper I looked into her Facebook page, I figured out her mother was a professor who worked at a prestigious college in Michigan and her father was a reputable doctor. As I stared at a picture of Porsha, my mind worried. It didn't make sense how she'd ended up dead. Statistically, she'd come from a great background, her parents had financial stability, and she'd graduated with a degree in science from a great university and could have been very successful. How did this happen? I asked myself. Who the hell had done this to her? And why?

I closed my laptop and began to worry about Karrine. I didn't want Karrine around Queen or Jacob, but Karrine seemed already to be caught up in their web of deceit. She was sleeping around with Queen and Jacob, and she was always trying to be at every event that involved them. I couldn't just tell Karrine what I knew; she was already too brainwashed by Queen. I had to finesse my way into getting Karrine to leave the elite crew alone, but I knew it would be hard.

Chapter Five
Wicked

The following morning, I made coffee and breakfast for Karrine, who had a crazy hangover. She sat at my dining room glass table, slouched over with her head pressed against a cold bottle of water. I chuckled and gave Karrine a plate of greasy food: sausages, bacon, eggs, potatoes, and toast. Karrine ate the food quickly then lay down on the sofa. I gave her two aspirin and she fell asleep again.

The second time Karrine woke up, I was in the kitchen cooking; it was eight o'clock at night. Karrine came into the kitchen, sat at the table, and I gave her some more coffee to wake her up a little.

"Ewww, I don't want this shit," she said.

"You need it, Karrine; you have a hangover."

Karrine sipped the coffee and made awkward faces, indicating the coffee was nasty and bitter. I laughed at her faces and teased her for drinking so much the previous night. I made Karrine a plate of the food I'd cooked: collard greens, fried chicken, mac-and-cheese, and cornbread. This time, she didn't devour the food; she ate it slowly like she normally did. Karrine's cellphone started to ring and I looked at the name on her cellphone; it was Queen. I snatched Karrine's cellphone away and declined Queen's call, sending the call to voicemail.

"Why'd you do that?" she asked.

"Because that bitch Queen is sneaky; I don't like her."

"Lauren, she's good people."

"How much do you know about her, K?"

"Lauren, you haven't even given her a chance. She's cool and she likes you. She always asks about you and if you're okay."

I folded my arms and twisted my lips up. Karrine chuckled and started to eat her food.

"If you know so much about her, why did her friend Porsha Dewey come up missing?"

"Porsha Dewey was murdered and thrown into the Detroit River. What does that have to do with Queen?"

"Did Queen tell you about her?"

"Yeah, she did. Queen and Porsha were friends at one point. I guess Porsha was trying to steal Jacob from Queen, so Queen basically cut her off as a friend. Then she came up missing."

"Right. Porsha tried to steal Jacob, or maybe it was the other way around. Queen is a liar, Karrine; why can't you see that? You're being very dumb right now by trusting her. The bitch is insane; she and Danielle are crazy."

Karrine rose to her feet, grabbed her cellphone, and started putting on her heels. She snatched her keys off the table and stormed out the door. I followed behind her as she walked to her car. She seemed vexed and frustrated that I was talking about Queen, but I was only trying to protect her—or ending up dead because of Queen.

"WAIT, KARRINE!" I yelled out.

"No! I can make my own decisions and pick my own friends. I'm having fun right now; I enjoy being around the elites. My business is thriving, I'm thirty-five, and I'm gorgeous. Let me live my life. You aren't my mother, Lauren. You're supposed to be my best friend. Stop trying to play the mother role because, frankly, I'm getting sick and tired of it."

"That's what I'm doing now, being your friend."

"No, Lauren, you're judging me right now. Yet, you slept with Drew, and now you want to play like you have all your ducks in a fucking row. You don't! Let me enjoy this moment."

"Don't say I didn't warn you."

Karrine got in her car and drove off. I was left outside in the dark, feeling witless and abandoned. I didn't mean to upset Karrine. I just wanted her to be smart about the people in her life.

I arrived at work the following day, and Karrine was there before me, helping clients. I was slightly astounded. Normally, she would be the last person to show up for work. Karrine and I walked around the store not speaking to one another and the other sales associates noticed. The tension was thick and I didn't want it to last any longer, so I pulled Karrine to the side and apologized to her. She accepted and we moved past it, and although Karrine and I were back cool, it still bothered me that she was hanging out with Queen.

I tried my best to get Queen out my head, but something wasn't sitting right about her. Karrine's friendship meant a lot to me and the best way for me to keep her close was to not get on her nerves about Queen. I would have to do my investigation on Queen right up under Karrine's nose. I knew that was the wrong thing to do, that I shouldn't spy on my best friend, but I didn't have a choice.

I decided to walk to the deli down the street from the clothing store. The sun was out and the temperature was eight-two degrees; it felt lovely. I purchased my food and started to walk back to the clothing store. Suddenly, a silver Rolls Royce pulled next to me. I stopped for a moment, trying to see who was inside, but all the windows were tinted. I kept walking, and the driver pulled up to the curb and got out the Rolls Royce. He was dressed in a suit like a chauffeur. He opened the back door and Drew stepped out the car. I rolled my eyes, exhaled, and started to speed walk. Drew trailed behind me as his chauffeur got back inside of the car, and slowly drove the car to stay near us.

"What do you want?" I asked.

"I owe you an apology. You have to forgive me. I didn't mean for things to unravel the way they did," he said.

I stopped walking and glared at Drew.

"Well, it's kind of too late. You had your bitch stalking me and making accusations that she's your wife and all this other bullshit,"

"Danielle wants to marry me so badly. She wants me to wife her and plan this happily-ever-after life with her, but I don't want her and she knows it. She's threatened by you. She knows I'm attracted to you and she's jealous."

I nodded. "I agree, so please keep her in check. She swears I want you; just handle her for me and we're even," I said.

"You didn't like the night we spent together, Lauren?"

I exhaled. "That night we spent together was well-needed and fulfilling. It wasn't a relationship and it isn't going to be a thing we continue. I was vulnerable and needed some stress release, and you were there to fill that void. That's all it was and will ever be! Why can't you or that psychotic bitch understand that? Seriously, why?"

Drew burst out laughing. "She is a little nuts, right? I do have that kind of effect on women," he said, still being playful.

"Yeah, whatever... I'm not dealing with this," I said, walking away from Drew.

Drew chased after me, and gently gripped my right arm. "All right, all right... sorry; I really am sorry. Danielle isn't my wife and I never promised her marriage. Let me make it up to you; let me take you out on a date. I promise I'll be on my best behavior."

"Uh... Nope, not going to happen," I said, walking away.

"Come on, Lauren; we can talk about anything."

I stopped and thought about the girl Porsha and realized I'd struck gold. The only way I was going to know exactly what happened to Porsha was if I got the inside scoop from within their little clique. I knew it wasn't going to be easy getting information out of Drew, but he was my only source.

"Deal. Nine o'clock sharp at the Mega Steakhouse in Downtown Royal Oak."

"Ahh, expensive tastes."

"Sure, whatever; I'll meet your there."

Drew was sexy, but I didn't trust him. He was very intriguing, but I knew he had a playboy reputation.

"I can't pick you up?"

"Hell no!"

He smiled and I smiled back; when I realized I was smiling with him, I stopped. Keithly might have been right. I was attracted to Drew, but I wasn't a fool. I wasn't going to give him the opportunity again to make me look moronic. I was going to play a role just like he had been doing when he and I first met.

"Listen, Lauren, I'm not trying to hurt you or play you. I was definitely wrong for acting like I didn't know you in front of Danielle, but trust me, she is not my woman or my wife. She and I had an understanding, but that was broken when she showed me, she was untrustworthy."

"Oh, did the bitch cheat on you? Or wait, did she break your heart and sleep with one of your friends?"

"Nothing like that. Like I said before, she was never my woman, but I'll see you tonight."

Drew kissed the back of my hand and walked back to his Rolls Royce. His driver opened the door for him, and when they were both back in the car, the Rolls Royce slowly pulled away from the curb. When I arrived back at the store, I didn't tell Karrine anything. I wanted to keep Drew and I a secret. The day slowly went by, and Karrine and I were back to laughing and being silly.

Queen came through the doors. It was thirty minutes before the store closed and we were closing down for the night. Karrine and Queen talked while I helped the girls clean up the store. Karrine ran to the back for a moment and I was approached by Queen.

"Hey, Lauren," she said.

"Hey, Queen," I replied. I wanted to keep it friendly.

"Listen, I know you think I'm stealing Karrine away from you and I take it you really don't care for me, but I care about Karrine, just as much as you do. She is my friend."

Queen was trying to play her little innocent act, but I wasn't buying it.

"Queen, you're right; I don't like you and I don't trust you. Just make sure when Karrine is around you, she's safe. You think you're so clever and you believe you have some kind of leverage because Karrine is fond of you, but I see through all of it. You aren't fooling me. In the meantime, we share a mutual friend, so let's just play nice and be cool for her. I mean since you're going to be in her life now, right?" I asked with a smirk on my face.

Queen pressed her lips together and stepped a little closer to me. I didn't move or flinch.

"You ain't nothing but a hoe. Drew fucked you and dismissed you with a quickness. You want my life, you want to be an elite just like me, but with that attitude, sweetie, it won't get you far. I run this city and my husband is a black billionaire tycoon, so you're right, you will play fair and I will spare you, only on Karrine's behalf. Believe it or not, bitch, Karrine is my friend, and you'd better get use to me because I will be around."

"Bitch, don't get cute right now. Don't let my pretty face and expensive taste fool you. I will slap the shit out of you. Watch your mouth and your back. If you play my sister, just know, I will be on your ass like a hawk. You can be her little friend, but always remember where her loyalty lies, understand?"

Karrine came out prancing from the back and Queen stepped back.

"Exactly," I mumbled.

Karrine approached and looked at both of us.

"Is everything all right?" she asked.

"Sure; Lauren and I were just having a talk about her Christian Louboutins," Queen replied.

"Oh, okay; well, Lauren, I'm about to get out of here. Queen is having a little get together at her house. You want to come?"

"No; I'll close up," I said, walking away.

Queen and Karrine walked out the store. I left the store and went home to get dressed for my date with Drew.

Chapter Six
The Consequences of Loyalty

I arrived at the restaurant and waited at the bar for Drew. He approached me with a dozen roses in his hand. There was no denying Drew's charm or looks because he had it all, no doubt about it. Drew and I walked over to a separate part of the restaurant, where there was only a table for two set up. Drew was engaging, captivating and a gentleman. He pulled out my seat for me and even ordered my food for me, but I wasn't there for his charm or his looks. I wanted to get some information out of him and I knew exactly where to start.

"It would have been nice if you'd told me how close you and Queen were. You know, her walking into your room the night of The Founders Ball and seeing me naked in your bed," I said, sipping my champagne.

Drew nodded. "I didn't know she was going to come to my suite, she just showed up. Queen is a very controlling and clever woman. She popped in on me and pushed her way through; she wanted to be nosy."

"Let me guess: you two have a past? Or is she trying her best to get you to marry Danielle?"

The waiter arrived with our food, then walked away, leaving Drew and me alone again.

"Both. Danielle and I met through Queen; I guess she and Queen are best friends. Maybe in the mix of Queen hooking Danielle and me up, she got a little jealous and she wanted me for herself, but Queen is Jacob's wife and I would never cross him. He and I are brothers; Jacob believed in me when no one else did."

"Ahh, interesting. Why don't you tell him about Queen? I mean, like you said, he is your brother, and if his wife is pushing up on you, maybe you should tell him."

Drew exhaled and nodded his head. "Queen is a very clever girl. Don't think it would be just that easy to write her off. She knows the ins-and-outs of things. You have to be five steps ahead of her because she always has backup plans. But let's not talk about her or Danielle; what about us? We had a great night after The Founders Ball."

"We did, but it was ruined because of you. You treated me like trash afterwards. It was very cunning and disrespectful of you, I'm a classy and well-respected woman. I deserve to be treated accordingly. You followed me around the ball trying to get my attention, then when I finally gave you my full attention, you played me and made me look crazy. Queen wasn't supposed to know about us."

"Can we please have a good night? I'm trying to show you something different. I'm not trying to play you or act discourteous. I just want a real shot with you, Lauren."

Drew reached over the table and grabbed my hand. I didn't want to fall for his tricks again because Drew was just as sneaky as Queen as far as I was concerned. I fell for his charm the night we slept together and he'd betrayed me by making me look stupid in front of Queen and Danielle. Drew had picked his side and he had sided with Queen, so I was going to play right along with him. I didn't trust him or want to be with him, but I needed to figure out Queen's motive regarding Karrine.

Not for one second did I believe Queen was Karrine's real friend. Queen was just too eager and determined to get Karrine as her friend. For the life of me, I couldn't get what Keithly had said out my head about Porsha. I had a motive of my own and I was going to get as much information as I could out of Drew. He knew Queen better than Karrine and I combined, so if Drew wanted to play this weak ass game, claiming he actually liked me, I was going to play along too.

"Okay, show me you do then, Drew."

"Anything you want, I got you."

We were done eating and I was ready to go home, but Drew insisted he had another surprise for me. We walked out the restaurant, and right in front was a beautiful horse-drawn carriage. The horse was white and the carriage was silver and bedazzled as if it had been designed for a princess. It looked like something out of a fairytale movie. My eyes gazed and I smiled from ear-to-ear. Drew looked at me with his gentle eyes and kissed me on the cheek. Then he grabbed my hand and we got in the carriage.

We wheeled around downtown Royal Oak and a lot of people took pictures of the beautiful horse and carriage; I also heard some of the locals calling out Drew's name. It was bliss. I felt like an actual celebrity being with him. It was interesting how people admired and gazed upon Drew, and he was very shy about it. He smiled and waved back at some of them, and even stepped out the carriage to greet them and take pictures.

I was in an awe, so taken back by his genuine spirit. This was the person I'd kissed the night of The Founders Ball, the genuine and sweet side of Drew. He didn't come off as cocky or aggressive. He wasn't shallow or rude like his business partner Jacob. He was different in and out, it seemed. He got back in the carriage and I gazed at him.

"Am I doing good or bad right now?" he asked.

"Good."

The night went on and I saw a deeper side of Drew. I was so impressed by his humbleness, but as we talked, I had to remind myself of what he had done and that his loyalty lay with Queen.

The carriage wheeled us back to the restaurant, and Drew and I said our good nights. He held me tightly and kissed my right ear over and over again. He smelled so good and he was so strong; I wanted to have sex with him in the car. My knees wobbled and my heartbeat rapidly. There was something so intriguing about Drew that I couldn't let go. I felt like I was falling for the okey-doke again; I had to stay focused. I gently pushed Drew off me and got in my car. He held my hand as I slid my body into my seat then kissed my hand.

"Good night, Lauren."

"Good night, Drew."

I swiftly sped off, leaving Drew. As I drove home, I wanted to turn around and go back to him. My cellphone started to buzz. It was Karrine calling; I quickly answered.

"Hey, K."

"Hey; I'm about to go to this club lounge in Royal Oak with Queen. They're having a celebration for closing a deal on a business plan. You want to come?"

Normally, I wouldn't go, but I knew if Queen and Jacob were there, Drew would be there too, and I wanted to see him again. I didn't know why, but I really wanted to see him.

I arrived at the club and there was a line outside the club. I called Karrine, and she came outside and grabbed me from the long line. It wasn't a typical kind of club. It was very chill and exclusive inside. When I arrived, Drew was there, standing next to Danielle. Queen gave a toast to Jacob for his success, and oddly, she was being very pleasant to me when she approached me. Drew and I locked eyes, and Danielle flexed her jaw. I guess my presence bothered her. Drew walked over to me, gave me a champagne glass, and filled my glass to the top.

"I didn't know you were going to be here," he said.

"I'm full of surprises."

Danielle's eyes darted between Drew and me, and it was so funny how mad she was. She walked over to the bar, I assumed trying to get Drew's attention, but he paid her no mind. It was weird seeing all Detroit's elite business owners in a laid back club. Normally, they were all in suits, acting as if they were better than the lower and middle classes.

It was getting late and I was officially tired. Karrine stayed with Queen, and Drew walked me to my car. This time he kissed me on the lips, and we didn't stop. We just kept kissing and kissing. We didn't care who saw us; we just had a make out session with no cares.

"Come to my place," he insisted.

I shook my head no, but he was insistent. He begged me repeatedly and I finally gave in. I followed Drew to his condo in West Bloomfield Hills, and we pulled into his driveway. As I sat there for a moment, I thought of the possibilities if I went inside of Drew's home. Of course, I was extremely attracted to him, and of course, I wanted to have sex with him. I knew I shouldn't, but his charm had won me over, and to be completely honest, I was horny.

Drew walked over to my car, opened the door for me, and I followed him inside. He had a luxury bachelor pad. Most of his furniture was black, and although it was simple and dull, it fit him just right. He lived in a three-floor condominium with a two-car garage and a balcony that faced the woods. I got comfortable by kicking off my heels and sitting on the sofa. I turned on the television and got caught up in reality television. Drew came down the stairs and sat next to me on the sofa. He stared at me and ran his fingers through my hair.

I leaned my head back and exhaled. I snuggled up next to Drew and we watched television until we both started yawning and stretching. I rose to my feet and started to put on my heels, but Drew stopped me and took me upstairs. I jumped in the shower then lay next to Drew in his bed. We didn't have sex; we just cuddled and enjoyed each other's company.

Drew's cellphone started to ring. He leaned over and looked at the screen; my eyes wandered over to his screen as well. It was Danielle calling him, but he ignored her call. Drew put his cellphone back down on the nightstand and his cellphone started to buzz again. This time he seemed more irked. He declined Danielle's call again and turned his cellphone off. I sat up in the bed and Drew sat up too. He looked at me, lost and confused, but I was curious to know his history with Danielle. I wondered why he was treating her so badly. I mean, I couldn't care less about her, but my curiosity had gotten the best of me.

"What is your history with her? She seems very attached to you. At first, I thought she only wanted you for financial stability, but it seems like it's much deeper between you two."

Drew exhaled and turned on the lamp next to his bed. "Danielle and I had an understanding. She and I were only friends with benefits. At first, she was a sweet girl, but she started to want to be like Queen so much; she wanted to do everything Queen did. The more I hung out with her, the more I realized how shallow and selfish she had become. She started thinking, since she hung with Queen and she was dating me, that she had some kind of privilege."

"Yeah, she does act that way. However, you said she did something that broke your trust. What was that?"

Drew smirked and leaned back and pressed his head against the headboard. "It's nothing. I just don't really like her," he said, brushing it off.

I nodded.

"Let's get some sleep," he said.

Drew turned off his lamp, and we fell asleep cuddled up next to each other.

I awakened to Drew next to me still asleep. I slid out the bed, and tried to quietly put on my clothes, but Drew woke up. He walked me to my car and kissed me on the cheek. I drove home with a smile on my face; it had been nice spending the night with him. My cellphone started to buzz in my purse. I stopped at the red light and dug into my purse to my find it. Karrine was calling me, but it stopped ringing. I brushed it off thinking she must have made a mistake by calling me.

I pulled into my driveway and Karrine's Bentley was parked in front of my house. She had a key to my house so I knew she was inside. I walked inside and Karrine was seated on my sofa in the dark. I opened the blinds and left the door open so the sun could shine through. She was quiet and seemed a little off. Her hair was a mess and her clothes were wrinkled and dirty like she had been playing in mud.

"K, what happened to you?"

"Lauren, I made a mistake and I don't know who else to turn to."

I placed my purse on the glass table and sat next to Karrine. Her eyes were red from crying and she was shaking.

"What's going on?"

She didn't respond.

"K, you're really freaking me out. What the hell is going on?"

Karrine shook her head and tears started to fall from her eyes.

"I think... I think I killed Jacob..." she said, looking at me.

"What?! What the fuck do you mean, you think, Karrine?" I asked, confused.

I heard a loud knock at my screen door and Karrine jumped back, afraid and nervous. I walked to the door and saw Queen standing there. I folded my arms and raised my right eyebrow.

"I know you weren't stupid enough to come here!" I said.

"Let me in, Lauren, please," she begged.

"Let her in, Lauren; she has to tell you," Karrine insisted and rushed past me to let Queen into my house.

I covered my face because all I wanted to do was slap Queen's ass down to the floor. I knew something was off about her, I knew she wasn't nothing but trouble, and I knew she was going to drag Karrine down with her.

"Tell me what?" I asked.

They both were quiet. Queen also was still in the same clothes she'd worn the previous night and she smelled like liquor. I wanted to vomit; it was so disgusting and infuriating to see her and smell her. Queen shut the front door and closed the blinds.

"Last night, after we left the lounge, Karrine, Jacob, and I went back to our house, and we all started drinking more. Jacob found out about some guy I was sleeping with, and he started pushing me and hitting me. I tried fighting back, but he was too strong; he slapped me to the floor. Karrine came up behind him and hit him over the head with a metal bat. Jacob hit his head on the dresser and collapsed on the floor. I tried and tried to wake him up. I tried throwing water on him, I tried hitting him, I tried everything..." Queen started crying.

"Did you guys call the police?" I asked.

"No, I was too afraid. I couldn't just tell on Karrine. He's dead because she hit him over the head," Queen said.

I looked over at Karrine, who was shook and crying. It broke my heart to see Karrine all shaken up. I bent down on my knees and was face level with Karrine. "K, is that what happened?"

Karrine didn't speak. She was quiet. I knew Karrine like the back of my hand, and I knew Karrine could never take another human life. Drunk or not, afraid or not, she just wouldn't.

"I just told you what happened, Lauren. Why the fuck don't you believe me?" Queen asked.

I quickly turned around. "BECAUSE YOU'RE SNEAKY, QUEEN. KARRINE WAS DOING JUST FINE UNTIL YOUR ASS CAME ALONG. NOW YOU'RE TELLING ME MY BEST FRIEND, WHO'VE I KNOWN SINCE I WAS SIXTEEN, KILLED SOMEONE? BITCH, PLEASE, I DON'T TRUST YOU." I yelled.

"Shhh... Keep your voice down," Queen said.

I leaned my head back, and my eyes welled up with tears. *'How could this happen?'* I asked myself over and over again. This was something right out of a movie. Karrine was my sister; she'd taken me in when I didn't have anyone. I couldn't just turn my back on her.

"I don't remember anything, Lauren," Karrine finally said.

I rose to my feet. "Where is his body?" I asked Queen.

"We buried him," she replied.

"Are you fucking kidding me right now? How are you going to cover this up? He isn't some homeless man off the street. This man owns companies. He's an elite. He golfs with the mayor for goodness sake!" I raged.

"Don't you think I thought of all this shit already, Lauren?! I didn't run to you, Karrine did, but now that you know, I need your help. I mean, she was the one who killed him!" Queen said, pointing at Karrine.

"Yeah, to help you!" I raged.

Karrine was stuck; she didn't move or flitch. I sat thinking of ways I could get Karrine out of it. She was my only concern. I couldn't just let her go to jail and I couldn't just let Queen manipulate Karrine into thinking she'd killed someone if Karrine wasn't fully sure she had. I needed to get Queen out of my house. I needed to be alone with Karrine so she could tell me the truth.

"Where did you bury him, Queen?"

"We buried him outside of Ohio; that way, no one can tie us to him. I can tell the cops he left last night to make a run without telling me where exactly he was going. If we plan this right, it can look like he went missing. I don't know, but something has to give."

I had to think fast, so I agreed.

"We can take his car and leave it somewhere near an abandoned area in Ohio, come back, and get our story straight. Queen, you have to keep your fucking mouth closed, and tomorrow, you have to report him missing. We have to go back and make sure we get rid of any evidence," I said.

Queen nodded. Karrine was so out of it, but I needed her to stay conscious. We all piled into Queen's BMW and drove to her home where she and Jacob stayed. We all went inside to wipe down everything and clean up to make things look normal. Karrine sat on the sofa in a daze, and as I cleaned, all I kept thinking about was the young girl Porsha. I knew Queen had probably concocted some kind of plan to have her murdered, I just knew it.

It blew my mind how tranquil and settled Queen was as we tried to make her home look normal. We wiped down my handprints and Karrine's handprints, and we gave Karrine an alibi. She was going to be at her mother's house, who was forgetful. We waited for it to get a little dark outside, and Queen and I drove Jacob's car to an urban neighborhood in Ohio while Karrine drove Queen's car behind us. I wanted to be in the car with Queen just in case she tried anything slick. I didn't trust Queen, never would, and Karrine and I wouldn't have been in this situation if she would have just listened to me.

There was no reason to chew Karrine out or make her feel worse than she already did. No matter what, I could never turn my back on Karrine. She was my best friend and she was willing to do anything for me. As her best friend, I had to return that loyalty. Of course, I felt stupid, and of course, I was afraid of the consequences, but my hands were tied. All I could think about was how Karrine had taken me in as a minor; after my mother went to jail, I never heard or saw her again. Karrine was my only family, and no matter what, I had to protect her, no matter how old she was or even how stupid and unthinkable the things she did were.

Things had been so different only a month ago. Karrine and I had been on our shit. Then Queen had come along with her wicked and dishonest ways. I looked at Queen as she drove. She was a beautiful woman, but she was a snake. Even God's most beautiful angel had betrayed him. That shows that beauty doesn't mean anything if the soul is wicked and tainted. I was completely disgusted. Queen was the devil in disguise.

Chapter Seven
Liar, Liar, Part Two

As we drove back after ditching Jacob's car, I felt sick to my stomach and told Karrine to pull over to the curb. I vomited all over the curb. My stomach burned and I felt ill. I couldn't believe I was an accessory to murder; this was all Queen's fault. I wish Karrine would have just listened to me. Queen was bad news from the start.

Queen dropped Karrine and me off at my house; we both were quiet. I went inside, took a shower, and went to bed. Karrine spent the night and slept in the guest bedroom. The following day, Karrine made breakfast and she had a clear head. She woke me up with orange juice and aspirin. She tried her best to make me feel better, but I didn't. We sat at the table in the dining room, our forks tapping the plate, our chewing the only sound. It was awkward, but I knew if I opened my mouth, nothing but horrible things would come out.

"Are you going to talk to me, Lauren?" she asked.

"I tried that, but you didn't listen. I told you she was bad news, and now you aren't even sure if you did or didn't kill him. What type of shit is this? You're a grown ass woman in your thirties and you let Queen manipulate you."

I threw my hands up, then dropped them on the table. My body was weary and my mind was drained. I needed more sleep and I needed more time to reflect on what had happened.

"Lauren, I know, but that night is a blur. I remember drinking, calling you to come with us, and I remember seeing you leave out with Drew. But, afterward, everything is a blur. I was having fun and I guess I blacked out."

"Yes, I get that part, but since when do you black out and kill someone? Are you sure that's what happened? You need to remember; our necks are on the line."

Karrine shook her head and placed her right hand on her head. "Lauren, I know Queen was pouring me hella shots, and they kept coming and coming. We were drinking so much; she just kept pouring them consistently."

"Okay, but did you see her drop anything in your drink or something, K?"

Karrine shook her head. "I just don't remember, Lauren. It's really weird that I don't. I normally can hold my liquor and I'm normally conscious of my decisions and aware of the people around me. It just doesn't make any sense."

"Well, we have to figure out what happened because we have less than forty-eight hours before the police find out. Jacob isn't someone who can just disappear without anyone looking for him. And that selfish bitch will do anything to keep herself in the clear."

Karrine slammed her hand down on the table. "Don't you think I know that now, Lauren?!" she raged.

I rose to my feet. "Yeah, I bet you do *now*," I said sarcastically.

I couldn't look at Karrine any longer. I was so frustrated and fed up with her.

"I'm calling it a day. I'll see you at the store tomorrow," I said and walked away.

A week had passed, and Karrine and I had started to drift apart. It was weird and awkward for a few days. She wasn't talking to me and I wasn't speaking to her; I felt so betrayed by her. Karrine and I normally spoke to each other every day, but since Jacob's death, our lives had changed. That whole week, questions about Jacob's whereabouts flashed on the news: reporters, policeman, and citizens had all gathered to find him. They looked all over Michigan assuming he was dead, but no one had found his body, which was a relief for me.

I sat on the edge of my bed in the dark, and as the television flashed from one scene to another, I started to cry. I felt guilty about Jacob's death, while, in the process of, protecting Karrine. I didn't know the guilt would eat at me. My cellphone started to ring. I grabbed it off my dresser and it was Drew calling me.

"Hey," I said.

"I've been calling you. How have you been?" he asked.

Drew had called me that whole week, but I didn't have the energy to talk to anyone.

"Good, just taking a nice little vacation," I replied.

"Oh, okay... Well, when can I see you again?"

"Today; I need to get out the house."

"Cool, meet me at my house."

I jumped in the shower and got dressed. I walked outside and the sun was shining so brightly and the warm breeze brushed against my skin. I saw children riding their bikes and running up and down the street. I saw families on their porches, other neighbors watering their grass, and others walking their dogs down the street. Even seeing all those people enjoying their lives, I was still deep down miserable and traumatized.

I drove in silence to Drew's house. When I pulled into the gated community he lived in, there were press and reporters out by the gate, but they weren't able to come through without authorization. Drew lived in a nice condo in a prestigious neighborhood, and the property manager couldn't have reporters and press out in their neighborhood disturbing their guests. Drew had told the guard I was coming, so once I showed my identification, the guard opened the gate let me through.

I got out my car and walked into his home. I walked upstairs, and as I bent the corner. He embraced me with a big bear hug, then gave me a kiss on the cheek. I was afraid to look Drew in the eye. I knew Jacob was like an older brother to him. It broke my heart that I knew the truth, but I had to keep my game face on. I couldn't give any sign that I knew more than I was supposed to.

"I've missed you so much, Lauren. Why haven't you returned any of my calls?" he asked, holding me closely to his chest.

"Sorry, just some family trouble, that's all."

"If you need anything, I got you."

Drew let me go and we sat down on the sofa. I turned on the television and more news about Jacob flashed on the television. Drew eyes were glued to the screen; he didn't blink. I swallowed my spit and quietly exhaled. I wanted to break down and cry. I just wanted all this shit to be over. Drew shook his head and turned off the television.

Drew didn't speak about Jacob, and I didn't ask about him either. I didn't want to bring any more attention to Jacob, so I quickly changed the subject. I started talking about the new business deal Drew had closed the night they were celebrating at the lounge in Royal Oak. Drew spoke so highly about his new business deal that his eyes danced as he went on and on about the money he was going to make.

Suddenly, there was a loud knock at Drew's front door. He and I looked at one another. He looked more nervous than I did. Drew rose to his feet and walked over to the door. He opened the door and two men in suits were standing there; one of the men showed him a badge.

"Hello, I'm Detective Carter. I would like to have a word with you about Jacob Armstrong," he said.

"Yes, but can we step outside? I have my girlfriend over," he responded.

"Completely understand, sir," Detective Carter replied.

Drew nodded, stepped outside, and closed the door behind him. I raised my right eyebrow, a little stunned. Drew and I weren't in a relationship, but he'd called me his *girlfriend* in front of the detectives. I tapped my freshly manicured nails against the rail and waited patiently for Drew to come back inside. It was flattering that he'd called me his girlfriend, but why would he if we hadn't talked about it and agreed on it? I watched closely as Drew spoke to the two men. I started to get nervous and wary of their conversation.

Suddenly, my cellphone started to ring; Karrine was calling, so I quickly answered.

"Hello."

"Lauren, they found Jacob's body!" she blurted out.

"What?!" I said, shocked and afraid.

It almost felt like my heart had dropped out my chest, my eyes welled up with tears, and for a moment, I couldn't breathe. I sat down on the sofa, beginning to feel nauseated and my palms starting to sweat.

"Yes, and I've been trying to call Queen, but she hasn't answered any of my calls. Lauren, I don't know what to do. What if the cops trace all this shit back to us?"

I placed my right hand on my forehead. "Calm down. When was the last time you heard from her?"

"Umm... Like two days ago, but she rushed me off the phone," Karrine said, with panic in her voice.

As I exhaled, I heard Drew close the door. I could hear his footsteps coming up the stairs.

"Meet me at my place in like, thirty minutes," I whispered.

I hung up the phone and started to act like I was watching television. Drew went upstairs to the third floor instead of coming to main floor that I was on. His cellphone started to ring on the table. I leaned over on the sofa and saw Queen's name pop up on his screen. I wondered what Queen and Drew had to talk about. That was when I remembered Drew had said Queen had a crush on him, but he'd made it very clear he didn't have feelings for Queen or Danielle. I wanted to answer Drew's cellphone, but I knew that would be inappropriate.

Drew came back down the stairs, and I quickly leaned back over to the opposite side of the sofa away from his cellphone. He seemed frustrated and kept slamming things down as he looked for something on the table. He grabbed his cellphone and his eyes widened. Then he went back upstairs and closed a door behind him. I followed behind him and he was in his office whispering on the phone with someone. I put my ear to the door, assuming he was talking to Queen because when he realized she'd called, his eyes had widened as if she wasn't supposed to reach out to him.

"I'm busy right now," he whispered.

"I know, I know; this shit is fucked up," he whispered.

I heard him say bye, and I quickly went back down the stairs and sat on the sofa. I heard Drew coming down the stairs. He walked over to me and started kissing me on my cheek and lips.

"Babe, I have to go. I have to handle some business," he said.

"What kind of business?" I asked.

"I basically have to clean up someone's mess."

Drew walked me to my car. For the first time since we'd met, Drew was edgy and anxious. Normally, he was composed and tranquil, but now, something deep was bothering him. Drew kissed me on my cheek, and I got in my car and slowly drove away. Oddly, Drew was still standing in his driveway as I drove away. It made me curious, so I parked my car between two huge trucks and walked back around the corner near Drew's condo. As I peeked around the corner, I saw a woman get out of a black Tahoe.

I couldn't see who she was because I wasn't close enough, so I moved closer, ducking and hiding between bushes and trees. The woman was Keithly, the same woman from the restaurant. I peered my eyes and deeply sighed. I was wrong to assume Drew had been talking to Queen because now that I saw Keithly, I felt he had been talking to her. Keithly gave Drew a yellow package and they walked into Drew's condominium.

I walked back to my car and drove home. I wanted to go back and bust in the door to ask both of them questions, but I knew if I wanted to get the whole truth, I would have to find a way to be discrete about it. I was weary and thwarted as I drove home. I felt lost and felt like the clock for Karrine's and my freedom was running out.

I pulled into my driveway, and Karrine was sitting on the porch with her head down. When I walked up to her, she looked like she had been crying; her eyes were puffy, her hair wasn't combed, and her clothes were wrinkled. She looked a complete mess. No matter what, Karrine was always dressed in designer and she always looked her best.

I gently pulled Karrine up and walked her into my house. I gave her some clothes and told her to take a shower. I made Karrine something to eat and gave her some tea. It broke my heart seeing her despondent and unhappy, because I knew it was eating her alive that she'd killed someone. I decided to take Karrine for a drive to get her mind off Jacob. We drove to Karrine's grandmother's grave, the same grandmother who'd left her the inheritance. Whenever Karrine talked about her grandmother, it was always about good things and it always brought her peace.

Karrine and I got into my car, and I started to drive down the street. We were on Joy Road, and as we turned the corner to get on the Southfield freeway, a car hit us on the passenger side where Karrine was seated. I checked to see if Karrine was okay. She was unconscious; her forehead had a knot on it and she was leaning back in the seat. I started to panic and for a moment I couldn't breathe. The man who'd hit us came over to my side of the car and asked if we were okay. I shook my head no and looked over at Karrine. I pulled out my cellphone and called an ambulance.

I yelled out Karrine's name over a dozen times, but she didn't move or speak. I checked for her pulse and it was still there. I put my ear up to her chest and felt her heart pumping. I exhaled and inhaled with tears in my eyes, and I prayed to

God that He would save Karrine. I begged and pleaded that He would make sure she was okay. I apologized to Him for my wrongdoings, and at that moment, I needed Him more than ever. The ambulance pulled up next to my car. They pulled Karrine out the car and quickly put her in the back of the ambulance. I grabbed my purse and Karrine's and left in the ambulance.

When we arrived at the hospital and they rushed Karrine into the ER, one of the nurses approached me and asked if I was okay. I felt fine, but she put her hand on my head and I saw blood on her hand when she withdrew it. She quickly pulled me into one of the rooms and took care of my wound. I guess I hadn't noticed how badly I was injured because of the adrenaline rush. I waited for Karrine in the lobby until one of the doctors came out and told me she was okay. I felt a weight lift off my chest; I could breathe much better now that she was okay.

After a few hours of observation to make sure she was okay, Karrine was released and we were able to leave. Karrine spent the night at my house. She slept in the guest room again and I slept on the sofa, watching television until I fell asleep.

"Lauren, wake up. I need to talk to you," Karrine said, waking me a short while later.

I jumped up and Karrine was standing over me.

"I'm starting to remember things from that night."

"Huh?" I said, confused and half sleep.

Karrine was up and pacing the floor with excitement in her eyes as she looked at me. I sat up and looked at Karrine.

"After the club, Queen and I stopped at another bar. She and I were drinking heavily. She was approached by some guy who said his name was Ronnie. They went to a private area and started talking to each other. I didn't pay them any mind. I just kept drinking—"

"Wait! Did you just say Ronnie? He knows Drew. He and Drew were talking the night of Queen's dinner."

"Yes, Ronnie." Karrine described his appearance. The way she described his features and accent, I knew we were talking about the same guy.

"Then Jacob came into the bar and yanked Queen away from Ronnie. Ronnie pushed Jacob and they started arguing. I walked over to the private area as they argued, trying to pull Queen away, but she kept trying to stop Jacob and Ronnie from fighting. One of Ronnie's bodyguards grabbed Ronnie and pulled him away. Jacob's two bodyguards rushed Karrine, Jacob, and me out the bar quickly and into the truck."

"So, were Queen and Ronnie messing around?"

Karrine nodded. Her eyes welled up with tears as she continued to explain.

"I remember, vaguely, Queen crying over Jacob catching her with Ronnie. I'd never seen her so afraid and nervous. I started asking Queen questions like who was Ronnie to her and why was Jacob so pissed. She told me that she and Ronnie were messing around, and I remember trying to get more information. The more I asked questions, the more Queen became vexed and irritated with me. She poured me a glass of champagne and told me to take an aspirin so my hangover wouldn't be so bad."

"Wait, an aspirin? You took an aspirin from Queen?"

"Yes; it was wrapped up in white paper towel."

I rose to my feet and put my right hand over my mouth. "Karrine, you were drugged; that's why your memory is so off. Maybe the car accident triggered some of that memory."

Karrine eyes widened.

"Finish the story. What else do you remember?"

Karrine closed her eyes and tried her best to regain her memory loss.

"Ummm... I remember seeing Jacob and Queen's house. I remember Jacob dragging Queen out the van by her hair. And, I remember fainting and waking up on the sofa. I could hear Jacob and Queen arguing. I heard glass smashing and I could hear Queen screaming. After that, I remember waking up in the bedroom to Queen crying and saying, 'What have you done?' That's all I remember, Lauren."

"Karrine, I don't think you killed Jacob."

Karrine started to panic, then she started to cry.

"No, Lauren. What if I heard them arguing, or what if I heard Jacob hit Queen, and I went up there to save her? What if? I don't remember enough to say if I did or didn't kill him."

"Yes, K, but what if you were just passed out on the sofa, and Queen blamed you?"

Karrine wiped her tears then rose to her feet. I slammed my hand down on the sofa, frustrated.

"What?" Karrine asked.

"We wiped away all the evidence. Queen knew what she was doing when she gave you that pill. Queen set you up. She put the blame on you so she would be in the clear."

Karrine and I both sat on the sofa, in a daze.

"Damn, this is crazy as hell. How the fuck am I going to prove my innocence?"

"There has to be something in that house, that ties Queen to Jacob's murder. There has to be some kind of paper trail or something."

Karrine and I sat up the rest of the night trying to connect the dots. I even told her about Drew and me and our secret affair. Karrine told me everything she knew about Queen, Jacob, Danielle, and Drew, but nothing was out of the ordinary. We still didn't have anything to pinpoint any of them, but now I knew where to start. I was going to start with Keithly.

Chapter Eight
Hidden Family Truth

I drove Karrine's car because mine was in the shop from the accident. I decided to take a small trip to the restaurant where Keithly worked. When I walked in, there were only a few customers in the restaurant. I assumed during the day their business was kind of slow. I walked over to the bar to see if Keithly was around. One of the bartenders informed me that Keithly no longer worked there. She'd quit about a week ago. The bartender walked away to assist other customers as I sat at the bar confused. I got up and went to use the ladies' room. As I washed my hands, I thought back to the night of Queen's birthday dinner.

That entire night had been weird to me. I'd thought it was pretty odd that Keithly trusted me enough to talk about The Elites. When she saw Drew, she'd freaked out, but now, she had been at his house giving him a package as if they had an arrangement. It just didn't make any sense to me. I needed to speak to Keithly. She was the only one who could help me bring my theories to a full circle. How could I get in contact with her? She'd quit and no one knew where she was, so I had no leads.

I dried my hands and walked out the ladies' room. I turned my head and saw Ronnie sitting down at a booth alone, eating. There were two big men standing by his booth whom I assumed worked for him. I watched closely as Ronnie talked on his cellphone and ate his food. I wanted to approach him so badly, but I knew if I went up to Ronnie, I would be asking for a lot of trouble.

"He is cute, isn't he?" a voice said from behind me.

I turned around and there was a man standing behind me. I nodded and chuckled.

"Girl, he comes in here all the time, and he always spends crazy money with his entourage. I wish he liked men because I would be all over that," he said, chuckling.

I burst out laughing. "What's your name?"

"Calvin, but on weekends after ten o'clock, I'm Vivica, honey."

I smiled. Calvin was funny and he seemed delightful. He was handsome and tall with a caramel skin tone, hazel eyes, and broad shoulders. When I looked down at his big hands, they were freshly manicured with a French tip. Calvin's nails put my coffin shaped nails to shame.

"What's your name?" he asked.

"Lauren. I stopped by to meet a friend here, but I guess she doesn't work here anymore."

"Girl, I already know who you're talking about."

"Who am I talking about?" I asked, curious to see if he really knew.

"Keithly. Thank God she's gone; she is such a troublemaker. I know a nice, coy girl like you isn't friends with a bitch like Keithly."

I smirked because he was right. Calvin rolled his eyes and started walking upstairs where other people were dining.

Calvin told me he was taking his lunch and I was more than welcome to join him. I agreed; I had nothing else to do, and most importantly, Calvin was my only lead. Thankfully, he was willing to spill all the good tea about Keithly. Calvin ordered his meal and I ordered mine. I was shocked that the waitress was attending to him. Normally, if an employee wanted to eat, they had to eat in the back of the restaurant and order their own food. I looked on Calvin's shirt and noticed it said manager underneath his name. That's when I knew why he was able to do whatever he wanted.

"Now, what do you want with Keithly?"

"I was here a few days back at a friend's dinner; her name is Queen—"

"Ohhh, so you're one of the elites of Detroit," he said, interrupting me.

"No, I'm not an elite. You have to be a billionaire to be an elite. I just know a few of them."

"And Keithly's sorry ass was telling you all about Porsha Dewey and her murder. Listen, honey, don't be fooled by Keithly and Queen. There's a hidden family tree between those two."

"Family tree? So, are they like cousins or sisters?"

Calvin shook his head with a smirk. "They're twin brother and sister, fraternal to be exact."

I choked on my wine. *"What?! Brother and sister?! Like same mom and dad brother and sister?!"*

"Yes. Now, between me and you, Keithly and I use to be best friends. She and I use to party and do so much shit together back when she was Keith. But once she had her surgery, she kind of wanted to distance herself, so no one would know she was a transgender. Queen and Keithly were never close; they've always argued and tried to outdo each other. It was actually comical sometimes."

The waitress was approaching our table with our food; Calvin stopped gossiping. The waitress placed our plates on the table, and when she walked away, Calvin started talking again.

"Keithly worked hard to get that surgery. She saved up and finally was able to afford it. Keithly didn't get that money from men or anything like that; she worked for it, unlike her cheap-ass sister Queen. Once Keithly got the surgery, Queen started to get jealous. Keithly looked twenty times better than Queen and Keithly started to gain attention from many people because of her looks. No one knew who she really was or that she was a transgender. Some of the elite men and women invited Keithly to speak and give out awards at The Founders Ball. Of course, Queen wasn't having it, so she threatened Keithly, that if she didn't leave the elites alone and go back to being a regular bartender, she would tell everyone she was a transgender."

I sipped my glass of wine as Calvin spoke. I started to feel bad for Keithly. It was hard to do something like that, and to have her own sister turn her back on her must have been hurtful.

"Keithly obeyed Queen and came back here and worked, and she became cool with Porsha Dewey who came here a lot with Jacob. Porsha was a sweet girl; she was one of the people who knew Keithly was a transgender. Porsha accepted her and treated her like a sister. Keithly and Porsha became so close that Keithly was able to stand up to Queen. Keithly started going to all the parties, balls, and private gatherings with Porsha, and when Queen saw Keithly at these places, she was pissed off."

"Wait. Keithly told me Porsha was dating Jacob, and Queen befriended Porsha to get close to Jacob."

"Not exactly. See, Porsha did mess around with Jacob, but that was all in fun, nothing serious. Porsha really liked Ronnie and we all know Queen is a hoe. Queen wants all the attention on her, she wants everyone to like her, and she doesn't care who she has to step on. Queen apparently has a little thing for Ronnie; they've come in here together a few times."

"What about Drew and Keithly?"

"Ahh... Drew and Keithly were never together nor did they have a sexual relationship. Drew is different; he isn't like the rest of the elites. He knows Keithly is a transgender too, but Drew likes real women. He made that clear a dozen times."

"So, Keithly and Drew don't mess around?"

"Hell no!"

I nodded.

"However, Drew is still an elite, and he is on the rise to become the next big thing. Jacob is dead and Drew was Jacob's business partner, so Drew will take over. These elite men and women will do anything to stay on top. Don't ever forget that!"

"What do you think happened to Jacob?"

Calvin exhaled. "Honestly, I don't know, but whoever did it will pay the price. Drew and the cops aren't going to stop until Jacob's case is solved. Jacob was a billionaire black tycoon out of Detroit who knew everyone. He had connections to the police and to people on the street."

My cellphone started to ring; Karrine was calling, so I stepped away from Calvin. She was in a panic. She told me she caught an Uber to her house, to get more clothes. Moments after she arrived home, the police were banging on her door. She was too afraid to answer, so she'd climbed out the window and ran. She'd caught a bus to the west side of Detroit. It was like my heart dropped into my stomach and I began to panic too. Karrine told me she would be waiting at the Coney Island on Plymouth. I told her to stay right there and I would be on my way to pick her up.

"I have to go, Calvin. Thank you for everything," I said, pulling cash out my purse.

Calvin shook his head. "Keep your money." He rose to his feet and gave me a hug. "Be careful out there. These people are powerful and they don't care that you're a woman. They will do anything to protect their brands and their families."

I swallowed my spit and felt like I was going to pop an eardrum. I knew what Calvin meant; he was letting me know there was a chance I could be killed. My mind started to race and I rushed out the restaurant and hopped in Karrine's car. As I rushed to get to her, I called Karrine to let her know I was only ten minutes away, but she didn't respond. I called her again, and again, she didn't respond. That's when I realized there was a strong possibility the police had caught up to her.

I arrived at the Coney Island and there were police cars everywhere. My heart was thumping through my chest. As I parked the car and got out, I knew there was a possibility I could get arrested too, but I wasn't going to leave my girl hanging. I walked up to the door and one of the police officers, who was standing outside of the restaurant by the door gently pulled me back. While a detective in all black, rushed out of the restaurant, and gently pulled me away from the building. I brushed passed the detective and shoved his arm away. I looked through the thick glass of the Coney Island restaurant and saw Karrine slouched over.

"KARRIIINNNEE!" I yelled out, crying.

"Calm down, please, I'm Detective James. Let's talk over here," the detective said, calmly, as he pulled me back.

"NO, PLEASE, THAT'S MY SISTER. IS SHE OKAY? PLEASE LET ME GET TO HER!" I screamed.

"Ma'am, calm down. You have to calm down," he said.

I tried pushing the detective away and I tried hitting him, but he was too strong. He pulled me away and walked me back to Karrine's car.

"Please, she's my sister. She's all I have, just let me see her," I cried, looking deep into his eyes.

The detective eyes welled up with tears and he wiped his tears away. "I'm sorry, ma'am, but she's dead."

"NO, PLEASE NOOOOO... SHE WAS MY ONLY FAMILY! SHE WAS ALL I HAD! PLEASE NOOOOO!" I screamed.

Detective James held me tightly and I could feel his heartbeat. His heart was racing and so was mine. It was almost like he could feel my pain; he could feel my heart breaking into pieces. My sister was gone. Karrine was dead. She was all I had left.

Chapter Nine
Try Sleeping with A Broken Heart

"Do you need anything? I have coffee and water," Detective James, asked.

I looked at him with no emotion.

"All right... Ummm, I'm going to go file some paperwork, then I'll take you home."

I just looked at him as walked away. I didn't mean to be discourteous, but my heart was broken. Karrine was dead. They told me she had been shot in the head. The witness didn't know who the person was nor could they give a good description of him. The only thing the witness knew was it was a man who'd come in and shot her. The man had walked into the Coney Island, looked directly at Karrine, and shot her in the head.

The thought of Karrine being afraid in that Coney Island made me cringe. Then some random man had come in the restaurant and killed her. My eyes welled up with tears; I just couldn't believe someone had done that to her.

Detective James came back, walked me out to his car, and drove me home. I was quiet the entire time as he tried to make small talk. I looked out the window as he passed houses, cars, and bike riders. When Detective James arrived at my house, he pulled into the driveway and I got out the car. Detective James followed behind me, walked up on my porch, and stared at me.

"Ummm... Your sister's car will be towed here in the morning," he said, his hazel eyes looking into my eyes.

I knew he felt bad about Karrine being murdered. I could see it all over his face.

"Thanks," I replied.

I shut the door and took off my clothes at the door. I walked to my bedroom and cried myself to sleep.

I awakened at four-thirty in the morning, walked into the kitchen, and poured a glass of wine. I looked at the picture of Karrine and me on the refrigerator. I smiled then I started to cry again. I exhaled and shook my head. I missed Karrine so much, I just couldn't believe she was dead. I walked back to my bedroom and pulled out all the pictures of Karrine and me and stared at each picture. I would have never thought this was how it would end. Everything was different now. The world didn't seem right now that Karrine was gone.

The following week, I made arrangements for Karrine's funeral. The sale associates from our store helped me as well by doing most of the work. It was very difficult for me to pick out the casket, what Karrine was going to wear, and even the proper place to rest her body. The girls came in handy. They helped me and talked me through every single detail. I was so appreciative of them for looking out for me because I just couldn't handle it.

I decided to go for a run after arranging Karrine's funeral. I was stressed and overwhelmed. Her funeral was the next day and I didn't know how I was going to go on with life without Karrine. It was driving me completely insane, so I ran around my neighborhood for at least an hour. Whenever I felt tired or lost my breath, I walked or just stopped and admired the sun. I had to think really hard. I felt lethargic and lost about what I should do. My heart was so empty, so damn empty, and it hurt so bad.

I ran back to my house and saw Detective James in my driveway. I rolled my eyes and continued jogging. He was sitting on my porch and I slowly walked up to him. He had two bottles of water sitting next to him; he gave me one and cracked open the other. I folded my arms and squinted my eyes at him. He was starting to really piss me off.

"Yes, Detective?"

"No need to get all upset. I asked your neighbor had she seen you and she told me you went for a jog. She's actually a sweet old lady; nice to have neighbors like that."

Detective James rose to his feet. He was definitely eye candy to me. I guess I hadn't been paying attention to his looks before. He was tall, with hazel eyes, copper tone skin, and huge muscles, and he towered over me with his six-foot-one height.

"A very nosy old lady, if I may add, but what are you doing here?"

"Umm—"

"Listen, if you're trying to take me out on a date, it's a no. I'm not looking for a relationship or a fuck buddy. I'm going through a crisis right now. I lost my best friend, who was my only family, and honestly, I don't feel like chitchatting with you," I said, cutting him off.

Detective James' mouth flew open and he blinked his eyes. He seemed a little disturbed and shocked that I had been so blunt with him, but I really didn't care for any company. I needed time to reflect; I needed space.

"I'm not trying to do any of that, Lauren."

"Then what?" I asked with anger in my voice.

"Alright, so I'm new at this... Your sister's case is my first murder case and maybe I'm having a hard time coping with this too. I'm sorry if I'm being a pest, but the look in your eyes and the way your heart was beating at that Coney Island broke me too. I just wanted to make sure you're okay; I'm not here to have sex or take you out."

I pressed my lips together and sighed. I felt bad for being bitchy toward Detective James. I shouldn't have assumed that was what he wanted from me.

"All men aren't the same, Lauren. This case has been hard for me to understand as well. Karrine's background and upbringing don't match the way she died. I read up on her; she came from money. How the hell did she end up at a Coney Island in the middle of Detroit dead?"

"That's what I'm trying to figure out too."

"Lauren, be honest with me: was Karrine in any trouble at all? Because the police were at her door earlier that day, and now all of a sudden, she's dead."

"Oh, were they?" I asked, playing dumb.

Detective James squinted his eyes at me and nodded. "Yes; she didn't tell you?"

I shook my head.

"They asked her about Jacob Armstrong's connection to her because they knew she and Jacob had a thing going on. I guess Jacob was one of those movers and shakers. He was very tight with a lot of judges, and they saw Jacob and Karrine messing around at one point. That's all it was; they just wanted to know if she'd heard from him."

I stepped back and turned around. My blood started to boil and I wanted to scream.

"Is everything okay?" he asked.

"Yes, everything is okay." I replied, as I turned around to look at Detective James.

"I'm going to look at her cellphone records and get back to you."

"Sure. I have to go inside. I'm tired and I need to get some rest."

I cringed as I shut the door behind me. Karrine had thought they were there to accuse her of the murder, so she'd run off. That's when I knew someone must have set her up. It just didn't make any sense, but I was going to get to the bottom of it once her funeral was over.

୨◆୧

The following day, after having made all the arrangements for Karrine, it was time to bury her in the ground. I sat on the edge of the bed in disbelief. It was time to bury my sister. I put on my clothes and walked out the front door. There were a dozen flower arrangements and some roses on my porch from my neighbors. My eyes welled up with tears but I didn't cry. I wanted to be strong for Karrine; I needed to be strong for her. Detective James pulled in front of my house, got out his car, and walked up to me.

"Good morning," he said.

"I don't have time for small talk."

"I understand and I'm not trying to bother you. I just stopped by to see if you were okay. I know today is Karrine's funeral."

"Thank you. I'm fine... Excuse me."

I walked past Detective James and walked over to the truck waiting for me to get inside. Detective James walked behind me and opened the truck door for me.

"Also, sorry to be a pest, but I have some information involving Karrine's case," he said.

"Oh, believe you me, we will talk about her case," I said, looking at Detective James.

His face went from relaxed and calm to disturbed and fret. I wasn't worried about him at that moment; I had to hurry to Karrine's funeral. When I arrived at the funeral home, there were many guests, including some of my family who I wasn't close with. They were there for support and I needed all the support I could get. The service was beautiful and I tried my best to stay strong. So many people talked about her smile, her grace, and her style.

Karrine was my own personal angel. She'd saved me when no one else was around. She didn't even know me back when she'd seen me at Fairlane Mall, out there sitting on the rock alone. Even when I'd told her I was okay and that my low-life mother would be there to pick me up, she'd waited, then came back for me when she saw me waiting even longer. Karrine had taken me under her wing and taken really good care of me until I was old enough to support myself.

That was our relationship. We'd had each other's back no matter what. We'd fought for each other no matter what. Now, somebody had the audacity to murder her like she was nothing. It drove me insane every time I thought about it, made me sick to my stomach. I missed Karrine so much and I would have done anything to get her back. I couldn't go back in time, couldn't reverse what had happened, so I had to take it to the chin like a champ, and I did.

After the funeral, as all the guests waited outside, I looked around and saw none of the elites at Karrine's funeral, not even Drew. Karrine's murder had flashed on the television nonstop and none of them had come to her funeral or called me to see what had happened. For some odd reason, they'd suddenly disappeared into thin air.

I was approached by Calvin with a hug and a kiss on the cheek. He held me tightly, and when I looked into his eyes, he was crying. I was astounded to see him because he and I had only one encounter, but surprisingly, he was being a friend, and for that, I appreciated him.

"Are you okay, honey?" he asked.

I looked around and wiped my tears. "I'm hanging in there."

"Well, let's finish out this funeral, and I'll get you a stiff drink."

I smiled. "I need it," I said, a smirk on my face and tears in my eyes.

Later on that night, friends, family, Calvin, and I all went to a bar in Royal Oak and had a few drinks on Karrine's behalf. We all laughed and shared stories about Karrine, while Calvin sat back and listened. As the girls shared their stories, I felt close to Karrine again. I smiled and cried as they talked about my best friend. Damn, I missed her so much. My eyes welled up with tears as I rose to my feet and lifted my glass.

"Let's make a toast," I said.

Everyone lifted their glasses.

"To the most beautiful, classy, unforgettable, crazy, and ambitious bitch I ever met, my big sister and best friend Karrine!" I said.

"CHEERS TO KARRINE!" they all yelled out.

Although Karrine was gone, her presence was still around. Now that her body had been laid to rest, I felt a little at ease. The hard part was over. I was able to breathe a little now. It seemed like everyone was celebrating her life, and honestly, that would be the way Karrine would have wanted it to go.

Chapter Ten
Savage Mode

Savage: of an animal or force of nature, fierce, violent, and uncontrolled.

I walked out the bar with a clear head, and as I approached my car, I saw a woman leaning on it. As I got closer to my car, I realized it was Keithly. She had her arms crossed and her hair was blowing in the wind. She looked like some kind of superhero or something, but that didn't faze me. I needed her to answer a few questions for me because I knew one of the elites knew who killed Karrine.

"I heard you were looking for me," she said.

"And here you are, in the flesh, leaning on my freshly-painted BMW; get off," I said with no emotion on my face.

"Listen, I know what you're thinking. Calvin was right about everything. Queen and I are brother and sister, and my surgery is real, and that bitch Queen has tried everything to keep me under wraps. She tried tricking me, lying to me, and threatening me, but I stayed strong. I'm sorry about your friend Lauren—if I could change it, I would—but I warned you about them. I told you they were savages."

"No, you told me what you wanted me to know. You didn't tell me the truth. You tampered with your story, and you left very important information out, Keithly, so spare me with your bullshit."

"What bullshit?" she asked, her eyes wide and serious.

"Porsha was messing around with Ronnie, and you were trying to become an elite too. You made it seem as if you despised the elites, but you wanted to be an elite. You didn't tell me that fucking part because you knew I would want to know why."

"YOU WANTED TO BE AN ELITE TOO!" she yelled.

"I WAS PUT IN A SITUATION BECAUSE OUR BUSINESS WAS THRIVING. KARRINE WANTED TO BE FRIENDS WITH THEM, NOT ME! " I yelled back.

Keithly sucked her teeth and rolled her eyes.

"What were you doing at Drew's house?" I asked.

Keithly eyes widened and she looked around.

"Drew knows about me, the real me, just like you do. He's never judged me for it. I was paying him back; that's the only reason why, I promise, Lauren. I need Drew to protect me and I know he can, so I wanted to make it clear to him I was on his side."

"Protect you? From who and what, Keithly?"

"Queen, obviously! That bitch wants me dead, just how she killed Jacob and Porsha. Queen is a fucking snake, and she will do anything to make sure she's in the clear."

"How do you know she killed Jacob?"

"Isn't it obvious? Queen wanted Jacob dead for money reasons. She wanted to collect her cash and leave Michigan, and that's what she's going to do. Queen framed your friend and made her believe she killed Jacob. She slipped her a pill, am I right? She did it to Porsha plenty of times and made Porsha do things she didn't want to do. I guess Porsha stood up to Queen and paid the price for it. It isn't rocket science; Queen killed Jacob because she wants to be with Ronnie."

Keithly was such a liar.

"You're such a coward," I said as I smirked and shook my head.

"How am I a coward? I'm telling you the truth; isn't that what you want?"

Although Keithly had come clean about a few things, I still wasn't buying her story. Queen wasn't that powerful and there was no reason Keithly should be afraid of her. It was such a cowardly move for a cowardly bitch.

"I just want to wipe my hands clean of this shit. I'm tired of running and hiding. I want to live in my truth. I love who I am and I want to show the world. I don't know who killed your friend, but I do know she didn't kill Jacob. I've paid my dues to these elite sons-of-bitches and I'm done"

"You have something up your sleeve, don't you? You're trying your best to make sure you're in the clear. You're a fucking liar! You've lied to me about everything. You didn't warn me at all, you didn't help me at all, and now you're going to walk away as if you've done your good deed for the day. That's not going to fly."

Keithly wasn't slick. It made me wary that she was trying so hard to clear her and Drew's names. In my mind, that was a guilty soul, someone trying their best and acting out to prove their innocence. Keithly turned around, her legs apart, and she folded her arms. She stared at me, looking guilty or as if she was hiding something.

"Did Drew send you here? Did you want to clear his name too? Is that why you're here?" I asked.

"No," she replied.

"Keithly, if you see Queen or Drew, tell them I'm coming for their asses. All you bitches are guilty until proven innocent, you got it? Now run and tell that!"

I got into my car and sped off, leaving Keithly behind in the parking lot. I understood Keithly was trying to clear her name, but that wasn't good enough for me. And, honestly, I didn't trust her or anyone else. I felt she was knew more about the night Jacob had been killed than she was letting on.

For the next two weeks, I didn't receive a phone call or text message from Drew. It didn't bother me at all. I kind of had been expecting it to happen, but as he went on with his life, I watched him closely. I followed him to all his events and parties. I stayed low and kept my eyes glued to him. Surprisingly, Danielle was on his arm as well. After Jacob's death and funeral, the city of Detroit had embraced Drew to take Jacob's place. It was even on the news how Drew had taken over Jacob's businesses, and they looked at Queen as some kind of lost and lonely widow.

Drew did press conferences and interviews about Jacob and how he felt it was his duty to honor Jacob and make him proud. Drew put on a fake smile and made it seem like he was an All-American type of man. He even had the audacity to have Danielle on his arm at every single function. Queen, who had been in hiding since Karrine's death, finally showed her face. She wore all black and cried every chance she had when the camera was on her. It was all so comical because the people of Detroit and the press believed their bullshit stories, tears, and promises.

After watching their pathetic asses for two weeks, I decided to go purchase a gun for safety purposes. I went to go see a childhood friend from back in the day; his name was Big Boi Chuck. He was known for his ruthless and senseless acts when it came to protecting his reputation. Chuck played no games, and many people respected him for how he'd gained his respect from others.

As I pulled in front of his house on the west side of Detroit on Dexter, I looked around my old childhood block. I reminisced about my grandmother, who wasn't alive anymore, and I also thought about Karrine and the day she'd saved my life.

"Well, well, well, if isn't Lauren. What brings you over here to the hood?" he asked.

I smiled and embraced him with a hug. "Need a favor and I'm willing to pay the price."

Chuck folded his arms and raised his right eyebrow. Cars and trucks drove past us, music blasting, while young kids rode their bikes up and down the street.

"What kind of favor?"

"I need to get a gun, but I don't want it to be traceable back to me."

"A gun?" he asked, shocked.

I nodded.

"Why do you need a gun? A girl like you should be married with a husband, not worried about dangerous shit like that."

"I know you heard about what happened to K. Someone killed her and I think I know the people who did it."

"I heard; sorry about your loss. I know that was your best friend, but I don't think you should do anything like that, Lauren. Let me take care of it."

I looked over at Chuck and shook my head. "No, it's personal, but I appreciate you for trying to help. Now, are you going to help me or not?"

Chuck saw that I was serious and gave me a gun that hadn't been licensed yet, so there was no way for the police to trace it back to me or Chuck. When I drove off with the gun in my purse, I knew I was taking a risk. I knew I could have been smart and let the police deal with Karrine's case, but there was a fire burning in my heart, and I felt like Drew and Queen had disrespected me for the last time. I knew if I took someone's life, I would have to deal with the consequences; however, I couldn't live my life knowing someone had gotten away with Karrine's murder. I knew, no matter what, the police would protect Queen and Drew. I knew they would have no problem putting up bail of a million dollars and getting high-priced lawyers, and those high-priced lawyers would lie and cheat to make sure Queen and Drew were free. I wasn't having it!

I received phone calls from Detective James, but I didn't answer. I was out trying to figure the best way to get to Drew and Queen. They always had bodyguards and entourages with them, no matter what. I knew I couldn't use my charm on Drew either, so I decided to stop at the Magnificent Steak House. I went over to the bar and ordered a shot of vodka. I looked over to my right and saw Ronnie, once again eating his food, but this time he wasn't on the phone.

I walked up to Ronnie's table and both of his big bodyguards stopped me. Ronnie looked at me and leaned back. He smirked and ordered the men to let me through. As I sat across from Ronnie in the booth, he pushed his plate away and put both his hands on the table. I leaned forward, raised my right eyebrow, and put both my hands on the table as well.

"Lauren? The pretty woman from the bar?" he said.

I nodded.

"What brings you here? Didn't your little boyfriend Drew want me to leave you alone?"

The waitress approached our table with two shots of vodka. I took the shot and gently placed the glass back on the table.

"Drew is *not* my boyfriend; I'm single."

Ronnie leaned back and leered at me with lust in his eyes. I flirted back with him. For the next twenty minutes, Ronnie and I talked and laughed. Once I was finished doing all my flirting, I closed the deal by kissing Ronnie on the lips. He invited me back to his bachelor pad near the restaurant. Ronnie ordered his bodyguards to give us some time alone and started to take off his shirt. I started to unzip my dress.

I pushed Ronnie down on the bed and tied his hands with his tie to the headboard. He leaned his head back and I climbed on top of him. I pulled out my silver pistol from the back of my bra strap and pointed it right at his head. Ronnie eyes widened and he pushed himself up, trying his best to get away from me, but he couldn't.

"What do you want? Money? I'll give you money. Just please don't kill me," he begged.

"I'm not going to kill you, but I need you to listen."

Ronnie nodded as sweat beads dripped from his face.

"Anything you want, baby, I got you," he said, panic in his voice.

I put the gun down on the bed near my leg. "I need you to get me close to Drew."

"What? Why? Hell no; I'm not doing that!"

"I'm not asking you; I'm telling you."

"You don't know who you're fucking with; I will fuck you up."

"Are you taking me for some kind of joke? I will blow your fucking brains out."

"It won't be easy to get you close to him. Drew is an elite and he has people looking out for him. If I cross Drew, I'm for sure dead; plus, he's a good friend of mine. When I tell him you're looking for him, he will make an example out of you," Ronnie said, a smirk on his face.

I raised my right eyebrow. I didn't like Ronnie's cocky attitude; he was testing me and I didn't like it.

"You're insane. My guys are right outside my door. They'll hear everything and you'll be dead before you can touch the hallway. Now, untie me and I just might spare you."

"You're right; I am insane." I swiftly pulled the gun up and shot Ronnie in the head.

The gun had a silencer, so his bodyguards didn't hear the shot go off. If I wasn't going to be able to get to Drew with ease, I was going to leave him a message. I wanted to let him know I was coming for him. I knew Drew had people protecting him, but I didn't care. I wanted justice for Karrine and I was going to get it by any means. I climbed out the window and slid my body to the other side of the tall building, I climbed through an open window in a hallway, walked out the back of the building, got in my car, and drove away.

I heard a loud knock at my door the next morning. I jumped out my bed and peeked out the window. Detective James was standing on my porch. I rolled my eyes, exhaled deeply, and opened the front door. Detective James had started to become a pest; he kept popping up at the wrong times. I understood he was trying to comfort me and help me through Karrine's death, but I needed space. I needed time to reflect on her death and deal with it in my own personal way.

Detective James walked into my house without asking if he could come in. He had his right hand on his hip next to his gun. Outside was another police car with two officers standing next to it. Detective James demanded both officers to come inside, both officers stood by my side. While, Detective James went through each room in my house and even checked the basement. I watched him as he hurried to each part of my house with my arms crossed and my eyes squinted at him, slightly confused.

"What are you doing?" I asked.

"It's clear," Detective James said, to the officers.

Both officers nodded and went back outside to wait for Detective James next order.

"We need to get you out of here," he said to me.

I placed my right hand on my right hip. "Why? What happened?

Detective James shook his head and looked down at the floor. "Ronnie DeVito was shot and killed last night."

My heart sank to my chest and I swallowed my spit. "Oh my goodness... Does anyone know who did it or anything?"

"No. His bodyguards saw a woman with him, but they say they didn't get the woman's name or a good look at her."

I slowly exhaled. "Why are you here?"

"A lot of the guys at the station think Ronnie DeVito's murder is associated with Jacob Armstrong and Karrine's as well. There's no proof just as of yet, but the guys at the station are taking these murders seriously, especially Jacob's. No offense, but the man had a lot of friends over at the station."

"None taken, but I'm a big girl and I can handle myself," I said, opening the front door so he could leave.

"We need to get you somewhere safe. If this is true and they come for you next, Lauren, I can't have your blood on my hands."

"Why would they come for me? Neither Jacob nor Ronnie had anything to do with me. They were elites and I'm not, and neither was Karrine, so how does this involve me?"

Detective James looked up at me, then walked over to the front door and closed it so the other officers wouldn't hear him.

"That's what I've been meaning to tell you. Someone contacted Karrine before she died. There were text messages from a random number telling her to go to the Coney Island. I think... " Detective James hesitated to get it out.

"You think what?" I asked, as my eyes welled up with tears.

"It wasn't a coincidence that Karrine was at that Coney Island. Someone set her up, someone wanted her at that Coney Island so they could kill her. There were rumors going around after her death at the station that Karrine was well on her way to becoming an elite."

"No, no way. Karrine liked to hang out with them, but she would have told me if she was becoming an elite."

"Are you sure about that? I understand you and her were close, but maybe there were things she just didn't tell you."

"There is no way Karrine would keep a secret from me. She and I were best friends; we were like sisters. If anything, she would have told me first. That just doesn't make any sense."

I sat down on the sofa, confused and hurt. I knew Karrine loved to hang out with the elites, and I knew there was a small part of her that wanted to be like them, but I felt Karrine would have told me if she was trying to become an elite. She'd never come to me about making a deal with anyone.

"Please, Lauren, let me take you somewhere else."

I respected Detective James for trying to keep me safe, but I was okay; I didn't need protection. But I wanted Detective James to think I was innocent, so I agreed and packed a few bags and followed him to the station.

Chapter Eleven
Consequences

As I followed Detective James to the station, I thought of Karrine and my mind raced as I tried to connect the dots in my head. I wanted so badly for all of this to end. I wanted Karrine back and I wished we'd never met Queen. As I drove, I realized she was the key to all of this mess. She was the reason Karrine was dead in my mind. It just wasn't fair.

We arrived at the station and Detective James tried his best to get me into a Witness Protection Program, but his chief felt there was no need for me to be in it. I wasn't a witness to any of the murders, neither were there any death threats against me. So, in their eyes, I was actually okay to be alone, but Detective James wanted to make sure I was safe. He walked over to me with his head down. I smirked because I thought it was adorable, he wanted to protect me so badly, but they were right. I was fine and no one was looking for me just yet.

"Sorry, Lauren, but I have another idea. You can stay at my place until this blows over."

"No; no, thank you. I'll just go back home."

"Please, Lauren. I have a two-bedroom, two-bathroom studio. It probably isn't what you're accustomed to, but it's safe and you won't be alone. Listen, I know you don't have family you can rely on or that you're close with. If something happened to you, I wouldn't know how to feel about it. It's my first murder case and I know I should keep my business face on, but I can't."

I looked at Detective James and his eyes said it all. He genuinely seemed very concerned about my safety.

"Let's talk about it over some lunch," I insisted.

Detective James nodded, and he and I went to a nearby diner in downtown Detroit. We ate and talked like everything was normal. He was even making me laugh with his jokes and stories. Detective James was loving and endearing and he spoke so highly of me. He admired my business-driven attitude, how strong I'd been since Karrine's death, and how sweet and genuine I was during lunch. As he spoke to me, I felt bad. Detective James didn't know the truth about me. All these good things he was saying about me weren't exactly the truth.

If Detective James knew I'd helped Karrine and Queen bury Jacob's body, and if he knew I was the psychopathic bitch who'd killed Ronnie, he wouldn't look at me the same, but I owed it to Karrine. She'd needed me during that time and I had to get revenge on the person who'd killed her. I wasn't sure if it was Ronnie, but I had to send a message to Drew. I needed him to get nervous. I wanted him to worry about who could have killed Ronnie. I knew Ronnie's death was eating Queen and Drew alive. It was only fair.

After a few more giggles and conversation, I decided to leave the diner. Detective James walked me to my car and gave me a hug afterward.

"If you feel lonely tonight, you know where to find me," he said, giving me a napkin with his address and personal cellphone number on it.

"Cool, when did you find the time to write this down?" I asked, looking down at the white napkin with smeared ink on it.

Detective James shrugged his shoulders, smiled then closed his eyes, as if, he was too shy to tell me.

"When you went to the ladies' room," He replied, looking back at me.

"Awww, Detective James, you care about me," I said, teasing him.

"Don't call me Detective. We're friends now right? So, call me Lance,"

"Okay, Lance, I have to go."

Lance opened my car door, and I slid my tiny frame into my seat. Lance leaned down and gave me a kiss, I smiled. Lance walked away and got into his car. I watched, closely, as my heart pounded uncontrollably. Lance had started to win me over; I loved the way he cared for me. I adored his charm, smile, and personality; he was different.

Suddenly, my cellphone started to buzz. It was Calvin calling and he wanted to gossip about his employees. I really wasn't interested in his conversation, I had my own personal business that was driving me crazy, but as Calvin spoke, he mentioned Queen's name. Apparently, Queen had come into the restaurant where he worked with a woman. I was confused because Queen hadn't been seen much in public since the police had found Jacob's body.

I was only five minutes away from the restaurant, still in the downtown area when Calvin called. So, as Calvin gossiped about whomever and whatever, I sat outside the restaurant where he worked, facing the restaurant. I waited patiently, and after about thirty minutes, Queen walked out the restaurant with Danielle by her side. I raised my right eyebrow as I watched them get into a black Tahoe.

Danielle got in the driver's side, while Queen got in the passenger side. I followed the Tahoe to Southfield, assuming Danielle was making another stop for Queen. The Tahoe pulled up to the curb in front of an apartment complex that wasn't gated and Queen got out. I watched closely as Queen talked to Danielle through the passenger window. I wondered what or who they were talking about. Queen walked away from the Tahoe toward the entrance to the building.

'Why is she going in there?'

Queen didn't pull out any keys to unlock the door; she just walked in. Once she was in the building, the Tahoe slowly pulled away from the curb. I watched closely through the glass and saw her go inside the first apartment on the left. I grabbed my gun out my purse and slid it between the waistband in the back of my pants and my belt so it wouldn't fall. I walked up the stairs and thought of all the things that could go wrong.

"Is it really worth it?" I mumbled to myself.

I closed my eyes for a second and saw Karrine's face in my head, and my eyes welled with tears. I opened my eyes and knew I was doing the right thing. I knew it was wrong to kill people, but Karrine was dead, and there were consequences and repercussions for killing someone I love. I exhaled.

I was at Queen's door, and for a moment, I just stood there. Ironically, Queen opened the door. She looked at me and I looked at her. She opened the door wider and ushered me in.

"Come on, get in here," she said, pulling me by my arm.

Queen shut the door behind her, then walked over to the glass table in her small, one-bedroom apartment. She pulled a pack of cigarettes out of her purse, lit one, then inhaled and exhaled. Queen looked like shit. Her eyes were puffy, her hair wasn't combed, and she looked thinner. Her body wasn't as curvy. Queen's hair didn't have its usual natural glow to it; her hair looked dry and brittle.

Queen seemed very off and I knew exactly why; she was heartbroken by Ronnie's death. I didn't care, Ronnie wasn't a friend of mine, and I didn't care because Queen hadn't protected Karrine liked I'd asked her to. Queen put out the cigarette and sat on the sofa.

"My, my, my, how the mighty has fallen," I said, looking around at her small apartment.

"Tell me about it," she said, rolling her eyes.

"What is a woman like you, Queen Armstrong, doing staying in a one bedroom, one-bathroom apartment? My living room and dining room are bigger than this."

"If you came here to talk shit about me, you can leave. I don't want to hear your smart remarks or comments. I know my life has changed. I'm not stupid!"

"Then what happened? You were talking so big and bad about your billionaire husband, trying to make me feel like shit because I didn't have a tycoon to take care of me, and look at you now, living like us regular folk."

Queen exhaled. "Jacob didn't leave me any money in his will. The son-of-a-bitch told his sister he'd never trusted me and that I was only after his money."

"Well, he was right, you were."

"No, I wasn't. I loved my husband, but once he started hitting me, cursing at me, and wanting other women to come into our bed with us, my love for him kind of dried up. I didn't want his ass anymore. He lied to me and treated me like an object. For a short period of time, I thought he cared—buying me gifts, making me feel like a queen when we were in public—but the man had demons. He was abusive and peevish. I don't miss his ass. I'm happy he's dead," she said, taking a shot of the vodka.

"Why weren't you returning Karrine's calls?"

"Because I was dealing with life. I was broke and getting questioned by the police, protecting our sorry asses. They kept coming to the house with different stories and theories about Jacob's death. Then, Jacob's personal banker took all the money I had left because, apparently, Jacob didn't want me to have nothing. He only left me the jewelry, purses, shoes, dresses, and five thousand dollars. Can you believe it?

Only five thousand dollars! He knew what I was accustomed to and he knew I needed him to live. Danielle put this apartment in her name and gave me a thousand dollars because Drew cut both of us off," she said, taking another shot of vodka.

"What? Why would he do that?"

Queen had tears in her eyes, and she started to cry and slur her words.

"Drew is now in Jacob's position. Jacob trusted Drew so much that he gave him his business and his money. Drew and Ronnie had gone into business together. They were planning something big behind Jacob's back and..." Queen hesitated.

"And what?" I asked, on the edge of my seat, anxious to hear what she had to say.

Queen shook her head as the tears fell down her cheeks. I placed my hand on my chest in disbelief. I braced myself for Queen's answer. Queen opened her mouth and my eyes widened.

"Drew and Ronnie wanted Jacob dead. Drew came to me about two months before The Founders Ball. He knew what I was going through with Jacob. He knew about the abuse, cheating, lies, and betrayal Jacob had done to me. One night at a gathering, Jacob slapped me to the floor in front of Drew, and Drew stood there in shock while Jacob walked out. Drew saw the hate and hurt in my eyes, and he knew I was so done with Jacob. The funny part is Jacob admired Drew and treated Drew like a brother. After Jacob slapped and belittled me one too many times, Drew and I quietly started our own little affair. One night, Drew talked me into killing Jacob but, of course, I couldn't personally kill him. I was so afraid of him. Karrine didn't kill Jacob and neither did I," Queen confessed.

I crossed my arms and leaned back on the sofa. My face was stone cold, and I wanted to slap the shit out of Queen so bad. But she was finally doing something I needed; she was confessing the truth.

"Proceed," I said.

Queen wiped her tears and rose to her feet. She walked over to one of her kitchen drawers, pulled out a yellow four-by-four envelope, and tossed it in my lap.

"What is this?" I asked, looking down.

"The night Jacob was killed; he and I had had a fight. He saw me all cuddled up with Ronnie at a bar and damn near bashed my head in. Karrine was asking me too many questions, so I gave her a pill to put her to sleep. Yes, I was wrong for that, but I had to follow through with the plan. Karrine passed out and was carried into the house and placed on the sofa by Jacob's bodyguards. His bodyguards left, and unbeknownst to Jacob, my twisted and sick sister Keithly came in."

"Keithly? You're lying! She said she cut all ties with you; she claims she's afraid of you."

"No. Keithly is insane; she's the one to be afraid of. She wanted my life so badly, and she was so jealous of me growing up. Our parents didn't accept her as a transgender, and my father turned his back on her as soon as she changed her appearance. Drew demanded that Keithly come to my house and kill Jacob. We were arguing upstairs while Karrine slept on the sofa; Jacob was hitting me and yelling at me. He bashed my head on floor over and over again. I saw Keithly come in behind Jacob and hit him over the head with a metal bat. Blood was everywhere and he was dead."

"Huh? What? This is too much right now. I'm tired of this fucking circle. You people are insane. There are so many twists and turns to this story. Why would Keithly do that? What is her point?" I asked as tears ran down my cheeks.

"Because Keithly wants to belong. What are you not understanding, Lauren? Keithly has been shut away her whole life. Our own family disowned her, and every time my father saw her, his face would twist up. When Drew gave her the opportunity to become an elite if she did just one simple thing, she took the fucking offer. She plays mind tricks; she is crazy. Why can't you believe that?"

"Because you're both the same; you're just as cunning and twisted."

Queen started crying. "It's the truth! She came in and killed Jacob and Drew told me to blame it on Karrine. Drew called Keithly not even five minutes after killing Jacob to make sure the job was done. This was all part of Drew's mind games; he manipulated Keithly into killing Jacob. I didn't know what to do, Lauren; my back was against the wall. If you open that envelope, you will see Keithly in my house, standing over Jacob's dead body, and me over in the corner frantic. We had cameras in our room because Jacob use to like to watch us have sex. I took the videos and screenshot them," she said, pointing at the envelope on my lap.

My eyes welled up with tears. I was so angry at Queen for not protecting Karrine. I exhaled and shook my head after hearing Queen's confession because Karrine had died thinking she'd really taken someone's life. She'd died with a burden on her heart for something she hadn't even done! It infuriated me. I'd known Karrine was innocent, but I hadn't been able to get her to believe she was innocent.

"Lauren, I'm sorry; I'm really sorry. Karrine was my friend and I loved her like a sister, but I was already in too deep. I'd already signed my life away to kill my own husband. I was so tired of being pushed, dragged, and belittled by that man. No matter what I did or said, I could never please him. I thought Drew had my back, I thought he was going to make my life easier, but the son-of-a-bitch made it worse."

I took a deep breath, trying my best to relax, but my blood was boiling. My palms were starting to sweat and my heart was beating rapidly.

"You call yourself her friend, yet you made her believe she'd killed someone. Karrine really cared about you and she really took up for you. I told her over and over again that you were a snake. I mean, you're just a low down, dirty snake in the grass, and you crossed her so coldly. With no cares in the world, you just crossed her."

"But-but... I didn't know what to do, Lauren. My back was against the wall, and if I had known Drew was setting Karrine up to be killed, I would have warned her. Drew was upset with her and... and... I'm just sorry, okay? I really shouldn't be telling you this," she said, with fear in her voice.

"Drew?"

"Yes, Drew. He wanted her out of the picture. Karrine and Drew had discussed her becoming an elite, but Karrine didn't want it. Drew asked her again after Jacob's death, but I guess she was so shaken up that she just didn't want to be a part of it. Drew felt he could control her by making her an elite, but when she turned it down, it was like a slap in his face."

"And how do you know about this?"

Queen exhaled. "Ronnie told me, and he said after Karrine turned it down, Drew demanded that Ronnie follow her and kill her, so that's what he did. Ronnie and Drew were like brothers. Ronnie was Drew's hitman, and when Drew told him to do something, Ronnie did it with no hesitation or regrets."

"Ronnie was a... hitman?" I asked, not able to speak properly.

"Yes, Ronnie was a hitman. He and Drew met in New York a few years back, and they called it 'a favor for a favor', meaning you do this for me and I'll do that for you. Most people thought Ronnie was some kind of businessman, but he was just a hitman people called to handle difficult clients."

I kept my composure as she spilled all the tea. Queen pulled out another envelope and tossed it to me.

"Here's all the info. I'm leaving this dirty-ass state. I can't be here anymore. I've paid my dues and I messed up, but I don't deserve to live like this and be treated this way."

I opened the envelopes and everything Queen confessed to me was true; it was all there in black and white. The pictures, Drew's offer for Karrine to become an elite, and her signature on the line declining the offer. My head was spinning, my heart was racing, and I was so pissed. Queen was still being selfish. She'd decided to turn over everything to me now because she wanted a clean slate, but I didn't care about that. She wanted me to clear her name.

It was all so typical of Queen, trying to befriend someone in a sticky situation, but what Queen failed to realize was that I wasn't Karrine. I couldn't be bought or tricked into liking someone or something so easily. Karrine was a forgiving soul, very gentle and sweet, and that's what made her special, that's what made her my best friend. But I wasn't buying the bullshit Queen was trying to offer.

"Now what?" she asked, looking at me.

"That day in Tags and Bags, I told you it was okay to be Karrine's friend, and honestly, for a moment, I had to step back and take my best friend's judgement into consideration about you. However, I did tell you that if something was to happen to her, I would be on your ass like a hawk."

Queen turned her nose up at me and rolled her eyes. She was still being a snotty, selfish bitch. She didn't care that Karrine was dead. I felt she'd used Karrine for her own personal gain.

"Your point? What are you going to do, Lauren? Tell the cops?"

I rose to my feet and quickly pulled out my pistol. Queen's eyes widened.

"Lauren..." she said, her right palm up. For the first time, I saw fear in Queen's eyes.

"You betrayed my best friend. I told you to make sure she was safe and you failed to do that. There are consequences for being disloyal."

With my pistol silenced, I fired it at Queen, putting a bullet through her head.

Chapter Twelve
Dog-Eat-Dog World

I stood over Queen's body with my heart racing, closed my eyes, and shook my head in disbelief. I sat down on the sofa and tried my best to analyze what I had just done. Queen was now my second murder. I understood I was wrong for killing these people, but I had to get revenge for Karrine. I convinced myself that I was doing the right thing. I exhaled and started to wipe down everything I touched; then I grabbed both envelopes off the sofa.

Before walking out the door, I looked back at Queen's lifeless body. Suddenly, her cellphone started to ring. I walked over to the table and saw it was Danielle calling. Danielle was irrelevant to me; she was just one of Queen's little minions. I was aiming for all the big shots. I existed Queen's apartment and walked over to my car. It was late now and the sun had gone down. The parking lot was filled with vehicles, but no one was outside. I swiftly got into my car and drove off.

I arrived home, quickly took a shower, and laid out everything in the envelopes I'd taken from Queen. I looked over every single detail, and as I read over Karrine's papers to become an elite, I cringed. I placed the papers on the sofa, went into the kitchen, and poured a glass of wine. As the jazz music played softly in the background, I broke down and cried. Karrine's death was really starting to take a toll on me; it was something I just couldn't let go of.

I wiped my tears and poured another glass of wine. I wanted revenge badly on Drew, and now that I'd killed Ronnie, who was his prodigy, and Queen, who was one of his side chicks, I felt like I was two steps ahead of him. I tried coming up with ideas to get close to Drew, but none of my ideas were good strategies. If I was going to get close to Drew, I would have to be really low-key and reticent with my movements. I knew it would be something I would have to finesse my way into.

I couldn't hire someone to get me close to Drew because it would be too risky if all my information got back to the police. Drew was an elite and elites were taken care of; everyone watched out for them. However, I still had my own personal leverage with the mayor. The store had been closed since Karrine's death, and I didn't want to continue the business without her.

"I'm going to sell the store," I mumbled, looking at the store keys on my kitchen countertop.

I knew the mayor would honor me for it, and I knew he would want to conduct some business with me. The mayor had always complimented our store space and the area; our store was a moneymaking catch. We were in a diverse area, and no matter what their race or nationality, clients came to our store and spent tons of cash. I knew Karrine would be turning over in her grave, but I knew she would want me to get justice for her more than anything.

Karrine didn't deserve to be murdered in cold blood. She had been tricked and manipulated into thinking they really cared about her. I only had four people on my list—Ronnie, Queen, Keithly, and Drew—and I'd gotten two of them out the way. Now it was time for me to tackle the other two.

৯◆ৎ

I arrived at the mayor's home in West Bloomfield Hills his original place of residence, before he became mayor. Sometimes, he stayed at The Manoogian Mansion when it was convenient for him. I drove my car to the entrance of the driveway, where one of his bodyguards approached my car. He had on an all-black suit with an earpiece. He talked into his sleeve and the iron gates opened. I drove up to the huge mansion and parked my car in an empty parking space. I fixed my hair and put on a little bit of lip gloss before entering.

The mayor and his wife had always been very generous to Karrine and me. He had always wanted to start his own real estate business and he needed a building to start with. The mayor was a smart man and he knew running the city of Detroit was something he didn't really want to continue. The mayor stepped outside with his beautiful wife Beverly standing directly next to him. Their grandchildren brushed past them as they played outside. They were like the black American dream and I admired that about them.

"Hello, Mr. Mayor," I said, extending my right arm.

"Please, Lauren, call me Joseph. How are you?" he asked.

Joseph welcomed me into his elegantly beautiful home, and he and I went to the back of the house outside. I walked along the beautiful outline of the golden bricks and looked out at Joseph's land that was as big as a football field. We sat down at a table where his lawyer was already seated and one of the bodyguards brought over a stack of papers. I pulled out my stack of papers and Joseph's lawyer looked over the paperwork as I looked over the paperwork he had for me.

Once all the paperwork was signed, Joseph dismissed his bodyguard and his lawyer.

We were greeted by one of Joseph's butlers who brought over a case of cigars; they were fresh and golden brown. Joseph offered me one of the cigars, but I declined his offer.

"You know, Lauren, I've always admired you and Karrine's drive. You two did an amazing job running that business, hands down!" he said, a smile on his face.

"Thank you, Mr. Mayor—I mean, Joseph. Well, this is a way for you to start your business plan to get into real estate. You have always said you wanted to step down and do something more of your speed, and not be so responsible for so much of Detroit."

"You have been listening to me after all these years," he said, nodding his head.

"Of course."

I nodded as he continued to talk.

"I wish there was something I could do about Karrine. She was a good woman, very strong and brilliant. I've known her for a very long time. I knew her grandmother, who owned that fabric business in Detroit," he said with tears in his eyes.

"I know; she told me all about it," I said as my eyes welled up with tears also.

"Be careful out there, Lauren. Some people are wolves in sheep's clothing."

I nodded as Joseph talked about the murders and the community of Detroit. I understood that Joseph had done all he could to revive the city of Detroit.

"Well, the elites try their best to give back," I said.

"Please! Those damn people think they're better than the community. They don't understand the struggle of Detroit. They don't understand how important it is to save Detroit and the youth. Of course, they give money to make themselves look good, and unfortunately, I've got to play along with them. But I'm tired; I want to rest and spend time with my family."

"Mr. Mayor—I mean, Joseph—were you an elite?"

"Hell no! I don't want to be involved with that mess. I've conducted business with those people, but I never got too close or invited them into my life. I was smart about it. I had to make sure my family was okay."

I felt my stomach turning and swallowed my spit. Joseph was hiding something, or he knew something.

"What are you hiding?" I asked, squinting my eyes.

"Jacob and Drew are deceivers. I saw how they conducted business. They always used an iron fist to get things done; those guys never played fair. They donated money for programs in the community yet encouraged violence and drugs in the community behind my back. I couldn't do much to stop them; they were powerful men, and Drew still is. I had to protect my family from it. That's why I want to just step down and not involve myself anymore. It's too shameful."

One of the Joseph's bodyguards approached the table. "Mr. Mayor, your car is waiting outside."

"I have a business meeting to attend, Lauren. It was nice having you here, and again, be careful."

I was escorted out with Joseph. He gave me a hug goodbye and got into the black Rolls Royce waiting for him. I walked over to my car and watched as the Rolls Royce stopped at the iron gates. The gates opened and I turned my head. Out of nowhere, I heard a loud explosion. I turned back toward the gates and the car Joseph was in was on fire. My mouth flew open as his wife Beverly came running outside and down the driveway. I ran after her as she tried to save her husband from the burning car.

Bodyguards rushed over to the Rolls Royce, and another guy grabbed Beverly and rushed her into the house. I started to cry as I watched the car burn. Joseph's body was burned and he was slouched over as if he had been shot. The fire department quickly arrived, and it was revealed that whomever had been driving the Rolls Royce must have gotten out the car. I placed my right hand on my chest because I knew the mayor had been set up and it had Drew's name written all over it.

I lay in my bed that night tossing and turning. I couldn't get the mayor's words out of my head. Now that he was dead, I assumed he'd known more than he'd led me to believe. It was unfortunate he'd had to lose his life. I felt bad for his family, but I guess it's just a dog-eat-dog world and no one is safe when dealing with reckless and selfish dogs.

Chapter Thirteen
Heart of Glass

The day of Mayor Joseph's funeral was tragic. His wife and children couldn't keep their composure. I stood in the back at the burial site as family members, friends, and other judicial members he'd worked with all stood around his grave. It was an eye-opening moment for me: It was me coming to accept the reality that Drew had a hit list. No one else suspected Drew because Drew made others do his dirty work.

A black Rolls Royce pulled along the curb. The chauffeur walked around to the rear left door and opened it. Drew stepped out the Rolls Royce in all-black. I moved to the opposite side of the crowd, so he wouldn't see me. A woman stepped out the car after him. She also wore all-black and had oval black sunglasses on. I couldn't tell who she was, but she had short hair and brown skin—until she took off her sunglasses and placed them in her purse. That's when I realized it was Danielle with Drew, but she had a new look.

Danielle had betrayed her friend Queen. Queen's understanding was Drew had cut ties with Danielle, but I guess they had been playing a little trick on Queen. Danielle was still prancing around with Drew; she wanted to belong so badly. She walked up to Beverly and gave her hug and a peck on the cheek. She wiped Beverly's tears and held her hand as if she was a friend to Beverly. It was so fake. Drew and Danielle stood directly next to Beverly and acted as if they had been friends for years. I knew that couldn't have been true simply because Joseph had admitted he'd kept his family away from the spotlight.

After the burial, I quickly walked over to my car and watched Drew and Danielle's every move. They got back into their Rolls Royce and drove away. I followed behind them as they made a stop at a five-star restaurant in West Bloomfield Hills close to Drew's home. I waited in my car, and once they were done and back in the Rolls Royce, I followed them again.

As I drove, I received a call from Beverly, who informed me that Drew was honoring Joseph next week. Beverly wanted me to come to the event. I told her I would be there. Beverly thanked me and went on about how she couldn't wait to see me.

I hung up with Beverly and watched as Drew and Danielle went inside a mansion. I assumed it was Drew's new home simply because I knew Danielle couldn't afford a home that big and expensive. I wanted to go inside the house and kill them both, but they had bodyguards; plus, I had to set up a way to frame Keithly for what she'd done. Keithly was the one who'd killed Jacob, then Queen had the nerve to go along with it. I still had the photos and the documentation to send Drew and Keithly to jail, but that would have been too damn easy. Drew had tons of money, so he would hire a good lawyer and get out with ease. Keithly, on the other hand, couldn't afford it and would be sent to jail.

I sat outside Drew's mansion for almost two hours. At exactly eight-fifteen, I decided I was going to kill Drew at Joseph's honor party. I drove off, and when I arrived home, Lance was sitting on my porch. I eased into the driveway and walked onto the porch where he sat with his head down. He kept tapping both of his feet against the concrete as if something was bothering him.

"What's wrong?" I asked.

Lance lifted his head, and I could see him clear as day because of the bright moon that was shining on us. He had tears in his eyes, and he closed his eyes trying to fight back the tears. I placed my hand on his shoulder and gave him a hug.

"It's going to be okay."

"This job... these people... sometimes, it can be a bit too much. Mayor Joseph's death is mind-blowing to me. He was a good man; I looked up to him. He was the one who pushed me into working for the law. Mayor Joseph always came to my school back when I was in high school and he always told me, 'We need more men like you on the streets.' I appreciate him for that, and now that he's dead, it just breaks my heart."

I was silent. I'd never met a man who felt comfortable enough to cry and break down in front of me. I didn't know what to say or do, but I knew Lance trusted me. I knew he felt he was able to count on me.

"The guys on the force are just treating it like another case; they don't care that he was set up. The man has a family. He has always did good for the community. He made Detroit an honorable city again."

"Yes, he was a good man, very true. He cared about the youth and he cared about his people from the hood. He reached out to us and gave people opportunities to succeed."

Lance nodded his head.

"Come inside; I'll whip you up something to eat."

Lance followed me into my house, and an hour later, I had dinner on the table: fried chicken, potatoes, mac-and-cheese, and cornbread. Lance swiftly ate the food and got seconds as well. He was an interesting soul. I admired his compassion and his heart. He was a man who wasn't afraid to break down, and he was so humble.

We sat on the sofa together and watched old classic movies. I leaned in and kissed him on his cheek. He looked at me with his beautiful eyes, and we stared at each other. I rolled my eyes and smirked, looking back at the television. Then Lance kissed me and one thing led to another. We were making our way to my bedroom, snatching off each other's clothes, and kissing each other's lips and neck.

"Are you sure about this?" he asked.

I pulled him closer to me and got on top of him. I leaned over to my nightstand, grabbed a condom, and put it on his dick. I gently pushed his dick into me and we both exhaled with relief. Lance grabbed my ass and pushed me down more and more until his dick was completely inside me. I screamed out and my eyes rolled to the back of my head. I leaned down to his face and kissed him while I rode his dick.

"Fuck!" he yelled out as his eyes rolled to the back of his head.

I moaned as we both came. I closed my eyes and collapsed on his chest. We kissed and I fell asleep on his chest.

The sun was beaming into my window. I turned over and looked at the clock; it was nine-thirty in the morning. Lance wasn't in bed with me, but his pants were still on the floor. I grabbed my cellphone, replied to my text messages, and called a few people back. I could smell something burning. I grabbed my silk white robe and put it on, walked into the kitchen, and couldn't believe my eyes. Lance was in my kitchen naked, cooking breakfast for me.

"What are you doing, crazy man?" I said as I burst out laughing.

I was laughing so hard my stomach started to ache. Lance started to laugh too. I fell to the floor because it was so damn funny that this man was in my kitchen cooking me breakfast booty-butt naked!

"I'm cooking!" he said with a huge Kool-Aid smile.

"You're about to burn my damn house down!" I said, still laughing.

On the stove was burnt sausages and eggs; even the toast was burnt.

"How can you burn toast?" I asked, dying laughing.

"Man, I'm trying."

He placed the burnt food on my plate and sat his naked ass on one of my chairs at the table.

"Go put on some boxers now; don't put your naked butt on my clean and beautiful chairs that cost me over a thousand dollars each."

Lance returned to my dining room table with his clothes on, and we laughed and ate the burnt breakfast. Two hours passed and we didn't even notice. Lance was late for work. When he rushed out, I cleaned the table and washed the dishes. As I cleaned the kitchen, I kept laughing because it was so charming of him to do something so sweet like that.

Later that week, Lance and I went out on a few dates. He took me to some nice restaurants and I even met a few of his colleagues from the police department; all of them were cool. After dinner one night, Lance and I walked back to his car so he could take me home. As I put my seatbelt on, Lance looked at me.

"You're a special woman."

I smiled. "Thank you."

"I know this may sound corny, but in the past few weeks since meeting you, I've realized that I genuinely love you."

My heart sank into my stomach and my palms started to sweat.

"You're so smart, beautiful, and funny—most women aren't funny—and you can cook and clean; you're the complete package."

I was shocked, but I played it off. "Thank you. I'm happy I met you too, and I love you as well."

In all honesty, I really did love Lance too, but he didn't know the truth about me: my lies, deceit, and that I'd killed two people so far. He was blinded by my looks, heart, and business-driven attitude. I felt butterflies in my stomach, not because he'd admitted his feelings toward me, but because he didn't know I was a murderer.

As Lance drove me home, we talked. I enjoyed him so much, but I felt so guilty. When we arrived at my house, Lance turned off his car. I took off my seatbelt and grabbed the handle, inching my way out the door. He grabbed my arm gently, pulled me back toward him, and gave me a hug and a kiss. I looked down, feeling unworthy to be in his presence.

"What's wrong? I didn't offend you by saying I love you, did I?"

"No, no, it's just I think we're better off as friends," I said.

The expression on his face went from excitement to sadness in a matter of seconds. "Why? I thought we were connecting."

"We were, but I'm not the woman for you. I'm still trying to find myself; I'm still trying to get my life together."

"I can help you with that."

I couldn't look in his eyes. I had to cut him off because I knew the truth about me, and those murders would get out soon. I had to break his heart now while the relationship was still young.

"I don't want to have a friendship or relationship with you!" I snapped.

"Wow! Just get out my car, Lauren."

I got out the car and walked to my porch. When I opened my front door, Lance slowly pulled away from the curb. I felt horrible for hurting him. I knew he was a good man and I knew it wouldn't be easy to run across another man like him again.

Chapter Fourteen
Revenge

I put my home on the market to be sold. It only took two days for a couple to make an offer. I packed my things up and sold a few of my belongings. The only thing left in my house was my bed, dresser, and a few paintings I'd purchased. I lay in bed that night feeling heartbroken again, but this time it was a combination of two losses. One was Karrine and the other was Lance. I didn't try calling him or anything because I knew it would cause a deeper issue that I wasn't ready to face.

I decided to drop off the copies of the pictures I'd taken from Queen at the police station. I drove by quickly and dropped off all the pictures and the documentation. I also kept copies in my car and in my house. I wanted to make sure I held on tightly to them. I knew those pictures were my only leverage. As I left, I saw Lance talking to one of his partners. He looked over at me then looked back at his partner. I felt like shit.

Another day passed and it was the night Drew was honoring Joseph. I decided to get ready for the function. My black hair was curled to perfection, I made sure my makeup was flawless, and my ruby red lipstick was from MAC. I pulled out my favorite deep red formal dress that stopped at my lower thigh and put on my open toe black heels. I looked in the mirror, admiring my look. It was unfortunate I was going to have to take someone's life looking this good.

I drove my BMW to the function. This time it was being held at the Edward Hotel in Dearborn by Fairlane Mall. As I drove through the entrance of Fairlane Mall, I cried just a little. All I kept thinking about was the day I'd met Karrine. After that day, she and I had never returned to Fairlane Mall for that reason. Back then, it used to remind me of my mother and that was why I'd never wanted to go back. Now it reminded me of losing my best friend. I pulled into the entrance of the Edward Hotel and parked my BMW close to the front.

I pulled out my pistol and put it in my black lace thigh holster, grabbed my clutch, and closed my door. The Edward Hotel was so large that it took me longer to get to the door than I'd thought. Once I arrived, the doormen were asking the guests their names and checking to make sure they had been invited. I entered through the double doors without any problems. I walked into the hotel and wandered around until the ceremony started. I had a few shots of Hennessy, but I was fine; I didn't feel drunk or tipsy.

As I looked up, I saw Keithly, Drew and Danielle going up in the elevator. The elevator stopped on the top floor, and I knew this was my only chance to get to them because I knew, once the ceremony was over Keithly, Drew and Danielle would leave swiftly.

I took another shot, went and got on the elevator, and went to the top floor behind the three of them. I looked over to my left and saw a housekeeping bin. As I went over, scanned the bin, and grabbed the master key, I heard someone getting off an elevator. I slid my body between a statue and the wall, and I saw one of Drew's bodyguards knocking on one of the hotel doors, B-505. Drew swung the door open, his pants unzipped, with an attitude. Two other women I'd never seen before walked out the room as Danielle stood behind Drew with only a thick, white robe on.

"Drew, the guests are waiting," the bodyguard said.

"Okay, I'll be down in a moment." He replied, calmly. Drew shut the door, and the bodyguard got on the elevator.

I was done waiting. My heart was thumping out my chest. My revenge started to tug at my heart and I wasn't afraid at all. I walked over to the hotel door, pulled out the master key, opened the door, and walked in. Drew was sitting on the sofa with a cigar in his hand while Danielle and Keithly sat at the bar. The way they were all sitting down comfortably made me feel that they were expecting me to be there.

"Well, well, well, the bitch who doesn't know how to stay in her place," Danielle said with a smirk on her face.

"Relax, Danielle," Drew said.

Danielle darted her eyes at Drew. She looked embarrassed that he'd told her to calm down.

"Yeah, bitch, listen to your master!" I said with a smile on face.

"I'm going to kill this bitch," Danielle said, getting out of her seat and charging at me.

Drew got up and stopped her by pushing her down on the sofa. "RELAX!" he yelled at her.

Drew sat back down on the sofa and told Danielle to go stand by Keithly, and the weak bitch did as she was told.

Drew's arrogant ass kept smoking his cigar. I wanted to shove it down his throat.

"Why did you kill Karrine? What did she do that was so awful to you?" I asked.

"Excuse us, ladies; this is a sight you don't want to see," Drew said, looking at Keithly and Danielle.

Both women walked out the room and closed the door behind them.

"You look amazing, Lauren; you really do," he said.

I folded my arms and leaned against the sofa as Drew tried dancing around my question.

"Drew, you must had mistaken me for one of your little followers. I just want to know why you killed Karrine!" I snapped.

Drew pulled out his pistol and sat it on the table. I watched him put out his cigar, then he leaned up.

"Because your friend was messy and stupid. She didn't know how to conduct business. She wanted to run behind Queen and Jacob, but I'm building an army and I need soldiers, not followers."

"Danielle and Keithly are followers, and Queen risked all of her fortune just to prove to you that she wasn't an enemy."

Drew eyes got really big and he looked up at me. "What are you talking about?"

"Oh, you know, Queen told me everything. She told me every single detail about how you wanted Jacob dead and how you guys tried blaming it on Karrine. Then she even told me you hired Keithly to kill Jacob."

"Stupid bitch opened her mouth."

Drew rose to his feet and poured a shot of Hennessy. Downstairs, there were cop cars all around the hotel. There was a helicopter flying above the building and someone was calling Drew's name. Drew ran over to the floor-to-ceiling windows, looked, and saw that everyone from the ceremony had been escorted out the building. The emergency button had been pressed, so the other guests were aware to evacuate the building.

"Yeah, I forgot to tell you: Queen had a little plan. She wanted to rat you and Keithly asses out to the police. She showed me the pictures and documents of all the sneaky and guileful shit you had hidden away, but since her life was cut short, I did the honors of dropping those pictures and documents off at the police department.

I started chuckling and grabbed the bottle of champagne and popped it open. "Good shit!" I said, looking at Drew.

He had fire in his eyes. I knew he wanted to rip me apart. I dared him to. I wanted nothing more than for him to try me. He didn't even know all the frustration and anger that had built up in me since Karrine's death. Drew walked back and forth as he tried to come up with a plan to get himself out the hotel.

"It's over, Drew."

"I'm not going to jail. I busted my ass too hard for this. Do you know how much shit I went through to get to where I am right now?! I am *not* going down like this. They're not about to tie me to all these murders. I refuse to have this happen to me!" he raged.

Drew started to sweat. The fire alarm had stopped, and I knew that meant the police department was on their way up to the suite Drew and I were in. Drew charged over to me, knocking me down on the floor. He slapped me in my face and blood was dripping down the right side of my mouth. I kicked Drew off me, he fell onto his back, and I pulled out my gun from my thigh holster.

"Get up!" I demanded.

Drew slowly rose to his feet. "You're not going to kill me. You don't have the balls!" he said, chuckling.

"You set up my best friend! She was all I had and you took her away from me!" I raged, tears in my eyes.

Drew just stood there looking at me with no emotion on his face. He didn't even care that he was the one who'd planted the seed for Karrine's murder.

"I'm sorry, Lauren. Please don't kill me," he suddenly cried out.

"Too late, bitch."

I shot Drew in the head and he fell to the floor. I stood over his body for a few seconds, then I heard the hotel room door open. I looked over and it was Lance. He stared at me as I stood over Drew's body, crying. He slowly entered the room, looking confused. Lance place his gun on his hip, and deeply sighed.

"I saw you; I saw you at the station yesterday. I wondered, why you were there, I kept thinking in my head constantly about these murders and how they were ironically happening. I Replayed, the video tape at the police station, and I know it was you that dropped off that yellow envelope." He said, closing the hotel door.

I didn't say anything, I just cried.

"Fuck!" he said, looking away from me.

I whipped my tears, I underestimated Lance, I thought he didn't know anything. But, the entire time, he had kept his eye closely on me.

"Those pictures and documents came from Jacob and Queen house," he continued. "I investigated a little more into Ronnie's death. I saw you on that video tape, at the restaurant speaking to Ronnie."

I was silently, I didn't move or blink. I just stared feeling ashamed and stupid. The look in Lance eyes burned through my soul, I felt so guilty.

"I know you killed them, Lauren." He said, looking down at Drew.

"Lance, I'm so sorry—"I replied, trying to get my words out.

Lance lifted his head walked over to me and started cleaning off my hands; then he cleaned off the gun I'd killed

Drew with. He put my gun on his left hip, because his gun was on his right hip.

"Get out of here!" he demanded.

"What? You know what I just did."

"Right. Now get the hell out of here. Sneak out the back and get far away from here because they will come after you next. Now go!"

I didn't ask any other questions. I hurried out the suite, down the back stairs, and walked out the back door. I rushed around to the front of the building and swiftly walked past police cars and reporters. Keithly was being arrested and put in the back of a police car as Danielle was being questioned by another cop.

My adrenaline was pumping so hard as I got into my car and sped off. My hands were shaking so badly that I could barely keep a grip on the wheel. I was too afraid to pull over, so I just kept driving. I stopped at my house and grabbed the rest of my luggage. Karrine and I had bought a nice condo in the Bahamas a few years back, and I was going to go there to live. I knew I couldn't stay in the United States anymore, so I'd decided to flee the county.

I boarded my flight and arrived in Miami, then waited five hours for my flight to the Bahamas. Before I boarded my flight to the Bahamas, I called Lance. The phone rang once and I ended the call. Suddenly, my cellphone started to ring and I felt butterflies in my stomach.

"Hello."

"Hey," he said.

I could hear the pain his voice and I felt awful.

"I'm sorry for everything and thank you for what you did back at the hotel."

"Say less... Take care, Lauren. I love you."

My eyes welled up with tears, and I closed my eyes as I tried to fight my love for Lance, but I couldn't.

"I love you too."

I ended the call and threw my cellphone in the garbage. I walked over to my gate, handed the gate agent my ticket, and got on the plane.

The End

Made in the USA
Monee, IL
26 July 2020

36874444R00090